THE BARN WALLS BECAME ALIVE WITH SCORCHING SHEETS OF FLAME . . .

"Up you go," Slocum told Mandy, grabbing her by the waist. But he never finished lifting her. Slim's head slammed into his back, throwing him forward. Slocum managed to twist himself around as flaming cinders sprayed over him. Slim braced himself and then launched himself at Slocum. Slocum drove a boot into Slim's shin and brought his knee up into his face.

Straightening up, Slocum heard Mandy scream. He started to turn just as she flung herself at him. Will fired. The bullet meant for Slocum caught Mandy in the back . . .

OTHER BOOKS BY JAKE LOGAN

RIDE, SLOCUM, RIDE
HANGING JUSTICE
SLOCUM AND THE WIDOW KATE
ACROSS THE RIO GRANDE
THE COMANCHE'S WOMAN
SLOCUM'S GOLD
BLOODY TRAIL TO TEXAS
NORTH TO DAKOTA
SLOCUM'S WOMAN
WHITE HELL
RIDE FOR REVENGE
OUTLAW BLOOD
MONTANA SHOWDOWN
SEE TEXAS AND DIE
IRON MUSTANG
SHOTGUNS FROM HELL
SLOCUM'S BLOOD
SLOCUM'S FIRE
SLOCUM'S REVENGE
SLOCUM'S HELL
SLOCUM'S GRAVE
DEAD MAN'S HAND
FIGHTING VENGEANCE
SLOCUM'S SLAUGHTER
ROUGHRIDER
SLOCUM'S RAGE
HELLFIRE
SLOCUM'S CODE
SLOCUM'S FLAG
SLOCUM'S RAID
SLOCUM'S RUN
BLAZING GUNS
SLOCUM'S GAMBLE
SLOCUM'S DEBT
SLOCUM AND THE MAD MAJOR
THE NECKTIE PARTY
THE CANYON BUNCH
SWAMP FOXES
LAW COMES TO COLD RAIN
SLOCUM'S DRIVE
JACKSON HOLE TROUBLE
SILVER CITY SHOOTOUT
SLOCUM AND THE LAW
APACHE SUNRISE
SLOCUM'S JUSTICE
NEBRASKA BURNOUT

JAKE LOGAN
SLOCUM AND THE CATTLE QUEEN

BERKLEY BOOKS, NEW YORK

SLOCUM AND THE CATTLE QUEEN

A Berkley Book / published by arrangement with
the author

PRINTING HISTORY
Berkley edition / September 1983

All rights reserved.
Copyright © 1983 by Jake Logan.
This book may not be reproduced in whole or in part,
by mimeograph or any other means, without permission.
For information address: The Berkley Publishing Group,
200 Madison Avenue, New York, NY 10016.

ISBN: 0-425-06338-0

A BERKLEY BOOK® TM 757,375
Berkley Books are published by The Berkley Publishing Group,
200 Madison Avenue, New York, N.Y. 10016.
The name "BERKLEY" and the stylized "B" with design
are trademarks belonging to Berkley Publishing Corporation.

PRINTED IN THE UNITED STATES OF AMERICA

1

It was a cold, wet night. Astride his spotted pony deep in the Absarokas, Slocum was trying not to think of other nights. Warmer, sultry nights, the air heavy with the scent of flowers from his mother's garden or filled with the sound of laughter and banter as the family and their friends sat around the front porch on the farmhouse at Slocum's Stand, while the fireflies chased each other in the darkness of the yard.

A sudden gust of wet, stinging wind brought Slocum back to the present, back out of that other world he had left so far behind him. It was all gone now, shattered and swept away by the flaming madness of a war that had almost succeeded in tearing the nation asunder.

Chuckling grimly to himself, Slocum hunched forward in his saddle against the chill, driving rain. He had miscalculated. This late in spring he had expected the Absarokas to be warmer, the land not

2 JAKE LOGAN

quite so inhospitable. That he had misjudged the season this badly was especially galling when he considered the bright desert sun, the hospitable adobe hut, the sunny face and the even warmer bosom he had left behind only a few short weeks ago.

Reaching a windswept crest, John Slocum shivered. Pulling his sheepskin jacket closer about his neck, he tugged his Stetson down further onto his forehead and gave his pony its head. For a while it followed the spine of the ridge, then started to pick its way down a narrow game trail. Soon Slocum found himself following a narrow trail, the steep, almost perpendicular walls of the towering mountains closing in on both sides of him. A while farther on, the trail came alive with the clamor of a swift, icy freshet. Abruptly, the torrent vanished off to his right, and the night grew silent again.

Slocum's descent was gradual but steady.

Like the road into hell.

The rain lessened a mile farther down the trail. Now the night was just cold instead of cold and wet. A slice of yellow moon appeared from behind the scudding clouds. It hung crookedly in the sky and gave precious little light, but it was something. Enormous boulders, some as big as houses, loomed ominously out of the night ahead of him, complicating the trail. But Slocum let the sure-footed pony find his own way past them.

Once beyond the boulders Slocum thought he could feel ahead of him the yawning emptiness of a large valley. He had not yet reached it; it was out there in the night somewhere waiting for him, still a good distance below the trail. He kept on, aware that he had rejoined the freshet he had come across earlier. Only now it had broadened into a powerful stream as it rushed beside him, eager to empty into the valley below.

He had left the wind behind, howling among the towering peaks. Unbuttoning his jacket, he thumbed his hat back off his forehead as the full, pungent aroma of a spring valley in full bloom came to him sweetly. It was a welcome of sorts, Slocum thought, and his spirits rose.

The trail left the stream and cut through a patch of timber, holding to a spiny ridge for a short while before plunging once again toward the valley below. Slocum leaned back in his saddle to ease his pony's load and drank in the smell of pine. In less than a mile, he reckoned, he should have reached the valley floor, but already, by the moon's dim light, he glimpsed broad parks and meadowlands on all sides.

These foothills, he knew, were the lush uplands the Crow and Blackfoot had once called their own. They had lost it all: first to the horse soldiers, then, finally and irrevocably, to the ranchers and cattlemen who had poured in after the buffalo were gone. John Slocum thought he could understand how they must have felt—how they must still feel. He too mourned a lost land and time.

These somber thoughts were broken into roughly when he caught the sound of shod hooves on stone off to his right. Turning his head quickly, he saw a cloud of horsemen descending upon him from a stand of timber just above the trail. As he pulled up swiftly and brought his pony around to meet them, he knew at once from the silent, grim manner in which the horsemen enveloped him that he was not welcome—that, for some reason or other, he was suspect.

Their leader, a powerful man with beetling black brows and coal-black eyes, put his horse alongside Slocum's. A big Colt was in his fist, the muzzle staring hungrily up at Slocum's face.

Beside him rode another rider, a slack-jawed jackel of a man with unkempt sandy hair sticking out from under his hat and a wild, unstable light in his eyes. He was the one who spoke first. "This be him, Slade, sure enough."

The man called Slade peered still closer at Slocum, as if he was not quite so sure as his partner. "Who're you, mister?" he growled.

"Who the hell is asking?" Slocum said.

This response momentarily set Slade back. He straightened in his saddle, his Colt still aimed at Slocum. "I'm doing the asking, damn it! If you're that U. S. marshal with them drovers, you might as well admit it. We got you cold, and their herd with it."

He smiled then and glanced quickly around at the ring of riders. There were a few soft barks of laughter. Slocum guessed Slade had at least ten, perhaps a dozen riders at his back.

"And if I deny it?" Slocum asked.

"Ain't no reason to believe you, if you did," said the slack-jawed fellow with a grin.

Slade turned impatiently on his sidekick. "Shut up, Jimmy. I'll handle this."

The blond fellow's face caved in as he slunk back like a dog that had just been kicked.

Slade looked quickly back at Slocum. "Where's your iron, Marshal?"

Slocum hesitated for a moment. The ring of riders moved a fraction closer. With a resigned shrug, Slocum indicated the cross-draw rig under his jacket.

"Get it, Jimmy," snapped Slade.

Jimmy reached in under Slocum's coat and pulled out the .44. As he did so, Slade reached over and withdrew Slocum's Winchester from the saddle scabbard. Slocum did not mention his other holster and .44 in the bag inside his bedroll. Not that it would be much help to him now.

"You're making a mistake, Slade," Slocum said reasonably. "I'm just riding on through. Whatever trouble you got in this valley is none of my business, and I'd like to keep it that way."

"There ain't no mistake, Marshal, and you know it. We been warned about you. Soon's we saw you on that spotted Indian pony we knew we had the right man. You got that from the Nez Percé. Right?"

There was no way Slocum could deny that. He shrugged. "What does that prove?"

Both Slade and Jimmy laughed at that. "Hell," said Jimmy eagerly, "half you drovers from Oregon ride them ponies. It's a dead giveaway."

"I rode up from the south. You saw the way I was coming."

"Real clever, coming from the south—over that

pass. Figured you might be able to scout us from the rear, did you? But it didn't fool us none, Marshal."

"I'll tell you just once. My name is Slocum. John Slocum. I am not a U. S. marshal."

"Then what're you doing here?"

"Riding through."

"Why?"

"God damn it, that's my business!"

Jimmy grinned. "No, it ain't, Marshal. Not any more it ain't."

One of the riders behind Slade spoke up softly. "It's getting late, Slade. The herd's due soon. If we're gonna take it before daybreak, we ain't got much time."

Nodding quickly, Slade waggled his gun at Slocum. "Dismount!" he ordered yanking his horse back so he could cover Slocum easier.

Slocum dismounted carefully. As soon as his feet touched the ground, he slapped the pony's rump. The crack of his open palm striking the pony's flank sounded almost like a gunshot. The horse bolted through the ring of riders and took off back up the trail. Now, if he got free of these men, he would at least have a mount and his extra gun—if he could overtake the pony.

Behind him, Slocum heard Jimmy curse. He turned to see the blond man fling himself off his horse and charge him. Slocum ducked away from a wild roundhouse, then came up punching, driving his right fist into Jimmy's slack jaw. Jimmy staggered back, but before Slocum could follow after him, a rope dropped over his shoulders and he was yanked cruelly to the ground. Before he could twist free, he was being dragged across the dew-wet field behind the dark cloud of riders.

Slocum was grateful that the ground was no harder than it was. But a moment later, while still struggling to free himself, he sideswiped a pine. The crack caused an explosion of lights deep inside his skull, and he lost consciousness.

He did not know how much later it was when he came to and felt his hands being tied roughly to his saddle horn. He opened his eyes and looked around him through pain-slitted eyes. It was still dark, but the clean smell of dawn was in the air. Looking down at his mount, he saw he was once more astride his pony. He did not need to look behind him to know that his bedroll was still tied snug to his cantle.

Beside him, the slack-jawed gent, his face swollen and his eyes mean, was holding the reins of his pony. As soon as he saw Slocum was conscious, he nodded with satisfaction.

"Be ready, Marshal," he said. "You got some hard riding to do."

"Damn you! I told you I am not a lawman."

"That's right. We didn't find no tin on you. But that don't matter now. Either way, you know too much."

A rider materialized out of the darkness ahead of them and cut toward them. As he pulled up, Slocum recognized him as the same man who had reminded Slade to hurry it up earlier.

"The herd's coming!" he called. "Move out."

"Okay, Mel!" Jimmy cried. "If I don't catch up to you in the valley, I'll ride on to Horse Peak and wait for you there. Tell Slade."

Mel nodded, wheeled his horse, and galloped back into the darkness. Jimmy moved out, tugging Slocum's pony after him. Slocum found it difficult to stay upright in the saddle. It was a combination of his hands being tied to the saddle horn and the residual grogginess from the blow to his head. It was still pounding mercilessly, but at this point the only way Slocum could treat it was with contempt. He was in danger of much more than a headache if he did not manage somehow to free himself from this crazy bunch.

Jimmy led his pony through a small patch of timber. Once they had reached the far side, Jimmy pulled up, drew his weapon, and stuck the barrel into Slocum's side.

"Keep your mouth shut, Slocum," Jimmy said, "and do as you're told. If you do, you might last longer."

They were facing a narrow funnel of meadowland that led gently down toward the valley. On the far side of the meadow there was a heavy stand of timber. Glancing beyond the timber and up the ponderous, steep-sided slope of the mountain, Slocum saw what appeared to be a break in the solid wall of jutting peaks that hemmed in this land. Here, undoubtedly, was a pass cutting through the mountains from the west. As the day brightened imperceptibly, Slocum thought he could make out a rough trail leading down from the pass and into the timber.

The ground began to tremble under his pony's hooves. At first, Slocum wondered if he were not imagining the sound—until he saw the herd materialize out of the timber. The air was suddenly vibrant with the bawling of protesting animals and with the deep, thundering rumble of their combined hooves.

Peering carefully into the grayness, Slocum picked out the two drovers riding point, the lead steers following them docilely. At least four men were riding swing on each side, while the rest of the drovers rode drag, prodding on the laggards. The entire herd trailed down out of the timber smoothly and began to follow down the narrow funnel of meadowland to the valley still far below. Slocum estimated the herd to contain close to two thousand head.

It was a pretty fair-sized trail herd from Oregon, fresh stock for the cattlemen on these high plains. Except that this time, Slocum realized at once, there was little or no likelihood that any of the cattlemen who had purchased this fresh breeding stock would see a hide or hair of it.

"Let's go!" said Jimmy, yanking Slocum's pony.

Lifting his own mount to a lope, Jimmy raced along the flank of the herd, keeping well in the shadows of the timber. Slowly he gained on it until he was almost to the lead steers, still pulling Slocum's pony along behind him. Abruptly, he changed direction and cut into the herd just behind the lead steers. The point riders did not look behind them, the pounding of the herd having effectively drowned out the staccato beat of their horses. The riders on the swing appeared not to have glimpsed them yet, either.

A shot ripped over the backs of the steers from the far side of the herd. Slocum saw one of the swing riders peel back off his horse. Half a dozen more shots came then from behind the herd and all along its flanks. Slocum glimpsed two more riders falling from their mounts as the dim light of the new day brought with it a deadly violence.

The herd behind Slocum lifted to a stampede. Like a multi-footed beast, it was in full stride in an instant. The meadow became a vast drum beating. Glancing back, Slocum saw the bobbing heads and swaying backs gaining on them as the herd fled in mindless panic before the continuing gunfire.

"So long, Slocum!" Jimmy shouted.

Firing back into the herd to slow the leaders, he dropped the reins of Slocum's pony and cut out of the path of the herd, leaving Slocum and his pony to the herd's pulverizing hooves. If Slocum went down before this mass of frantic beef, all that would remain of him would be small, bloody pieces. But already Slocum had bent his mouth to the swaying saddle horn and was ripping at the leather thongs that bound his wrists. He tasted blood and loosened a few teeth before he managed to slice through one strand.

But that was all he needed. He flexed mightily and yanked his wrists free of the saddle horn. In an instant he had tossed the leather thongs to one side and was leaning far over his pony's neck to grab the reins. The sudden shift of his weight forward almost brought the sure-footed animal to its knees, but the pony recovered and kept going. The reins in his grasp, Slocum straightened in his saddle and began to rowel frantically in an effort to keep ahead of the plunging herd, its awesome thunder gaining on him with every passing second.

It was light enough now for him to see a single boulder shouldering out of the meadowland just ahead of him. It was not as high as a man and no more than a couple of feet around, but it would have to do. He galloped directly toward it, flung himself from his pony, and dove for the boulder. His momentum carried him too far. Tumbling, he glanced up and saw a line of horns and wild eyes bearing down on him. He flung himself back to the boulder and scrunched down just as the herd thundered around it.

His back to the boulder, he watched the crazed animals swarm past, a tide of rocking backs and clacking horns. His own pony was still in sight. Without Slocum's weight to carry, he had been able to stay ahead of the herd, drifting to the right as he galloped. Slocum watched the animal break out ahead of the cattle at last and disappear into a line of timber above the meadow.

The boulder at his back shuddered as cattle slammed into it and veered aside. For a while he thought the boulder was going to be wrenched from the earth, but the danger passed abruptly as the last of the herd whipped on past. Keeping down, he saw Slade's men sweeping by, their eyes on the plunging tide of cattle ahead of them.

Waiting until Slade's men were out of sight, Slocum left the boulder and trotted across the meadow, his eye riveted to the spot where his pony had disappeared into the timber. Cutting into it, he found the pony grazing in a small clearing less than a hundred yards inside. Examining its flanks, he caught sight of a single break in its flesh where a horn had grazed it. It was only a scratch, but Slocum was anxious to take care of it as soon as he reached a town. This was a fine, sturdy mount that had taken him far—and this night it had saved his life.

He was reaching for his bedroll, anxious to get at his spare Colt, when he heard a sharp, angry voice behind him.

"All right, you son of a bitch! Freeze!"

2

Cursing softly to himself, Slocum turned.

A tall, resolute-looking fellow carrying a Winchester was stepping out of the timber. He was dressed in a sheepskin jacket, chaps, and riding boots. The man was obviously a working cowpuncher. Spilling down from under his battered Stetson, Slocum saw a tangle of coal-black curls. The fellow had a sharp blade of a nose and icy blue eyes that bored with angry resolve into Slocum's.

At once Slocum knew who he was: the leader of the drovers who had just lost their herd. And behind him, streaming through the timber, came what was left of the crew, their faces equally hard.

"I know what you're thinking," Slocum said easily, "but you're wrong."

The fellow kept his Winchester trained on Slocum. "Step away from your horse," he ordered.

Slocum did as he was told.

"I say we hang him, Harry!" cried a small, ferret-faced fellow who was pulling up beside the first.

"Damn it, Chino! Hold off a minute! I want to see what I can get from this son of a bitch."

Slocum cleared his throat. "I told you, you're making a mistake. I am not part of the gang that rustled your cattle. They tried to kill me. They thought I was a marshal you fellows had sent ahead."

"What marshal?"

"They had word one had been hired."

"Bullshit. We ain't hired no damn lawman." Harry's voice turned suddenly bitter. "Maybe we should've—but that don't matter now. We're staying in these here mountains all summer, if need be, until we find and string up every damn one of you bastards."

"That's right," his sidekick confirmed, his eyes glittering. "And we're starting right now, with you, mister."

"Search him, Chino," said Harry.

Chino stepped close and went over Slocum thoroughly. Finding nothing, he stepped back. "Must've dropped his iron when he went down," he said.

"All right," the trail boss told Slocum. "Lead that horse of yours out of here. We've got some dead to tend to before we see to you."

Realizing that further protest was useless, Slocum took the reins of his pony and led him back out through the timber, Chino sticking close beside him, the rest of the sullen crowd of drovers surrounding him as he moved. They were angry, bitter men. A less disciplined crew would have ripped into him by now, and Slocum was impressed by the self-control they were showing toward him. But that, of course, would end soon enough, he knew.

The drovers wrapped their three dead comrades in their slickers and buried them on the crest of a knoll overlooking the valley below. With the small, ferret-faced one called Chino Smith standing guard on him, Slocum leaned back against a pine and kept as still and as unobtrusive as he could manage throughout this somber business.

The unhappy drovers were just finishing with the burials when two riders Harry had sent after the herd returned with the news that, as before, it had been broken up into many small herds, each one funnelled off into the maze of canyons and valleys webbing these mountains. It would take one hell of a long time for them to follow each herd.

"I don't care how long it takes," Harry said grimly. "We've got the summer. We'll do it."

Slocum heard all this with a certain grim interest and then braced himself as these unhappy, frustrated men turned at last to deal with him. Watching them approach, Slocum decided he would have to do more than simply deny his guilt. There was no doubt they had seen him riding alongside Jimmy when the stampede began. To them it was apparent that Slocum, miscalculating, had let his mount get too close to the stampede, and had been overtaken by the plunging animals.

Harry pulled to a halt a few feet in front of Slocum. Slocum stepped away from the tree.

"Hanging me won't get you any closer to finding that herd," he told the trail boss.

"Maybe not," a fellow spoke up behind the boss, "but it'll sure as hell give us all satisfaction."

A graying, sharp-featured old puncher stepped forward with a rope in his hand. The hangman's knot was already fashioned. "Let's cut this short, Harry," he said. "This here's the first one we got, so let's make an example of him."

"Yeah," growled another. "Hang the son of a bitch high, like a banner."

"It'll make them bastards think again," someone else said tightly.

Chino snatched the rope eagerly from the old puncher and dropped the noose over Slocum's shoulders, pulling it tight.

"There's a limb over there," someone else said, pointing.

"Wait a minute," said Harry, peering curiously at Slocum. "Let's be damn sure we know what we're doing here, now." Addressing Slocum, he went on, "That horse you're ridin', mister—where'd you get it?"

"From a Nez Percé in Colorado four years ago."

"I don't believe that. You're from Oregon, and you was the one rode ahead and told them bastards which way we were coming."

"You're sure of that, are you?"

"Well, damn it! How in hell was it they were waiting for us like they was? I spent a month scoutin' that new trail over the mountains. Last time we lost a herd in these mountains it was fifty miles south of here. But here they were, waitin' for us. Someone from Oregon tipped them, and that's where you're from, judgin' from that pony of yours. So you must've been the one told them where to expect us."

Slocum nodded wearily. "Sure sounds logical. You need someone to blame, so I'm elected."

"Damn right!" snapped one of the men.

"Get his horse, someone," said Harry, turning away. It was obvious he hated what was coming almost as much as Slocum did.

Slocum's horse was brought. The heavy necktie still draped over his shoulder, Slocum pulled himself into his saddle. Chino grabbed the pony's reins and led the horse over to the tree they had selected. Slocum glanced up at it. The branch hanging out over the trail looked sturdy enough.

"Hold it," he said softly to Harry. "Maybe I can make a deal with you fellows."

Harry swung around quickly. Everyone looked warily and expectantly up at Slocum.

"Go on!" snapped Harry.

"You'll spend some time tracking each one of them herds. Like you said, most of the summer. And by then, I guarantee you, most of them trails will lead only to empty canyons and abandoned ranches. Let me take you through the mountains to the ranch where the herd comes together again. Hell, it won't take more'n a couple of days' ride."

Harry moved closer and glared at Slocum. "If you know where that ranch is, tell us how to get there, damn it!"

"Like hell. I want to live. I'll tell you nothing.

But I'll show you, if you take this damn tie off my neck. It's too heavy to wear comfortable."

Harry considered Slocum's words carefully before nodding. "All right," he said.

Chino piped up, disappointment evident in his tone. "You sure we can trust this son of a bitch? Maybe he's just trying to save his neck."

"If we hang him, we got nothing but a little satisfaction," Harry said. "This way, maybe we get the break we been looking for. I say let this bastard take us to their hideout."

"And if he don't," another man spoke up roughly, "he knows for damn sure he'll end up dancing on air."

The noose was flicked off Slocum's shoulders and someone handed his reins up to him. Harry mounted up swiftly and, unlimbering his Colt, nudged his mount alongside Slocum.

"Lead the way, mister," the trail boss said. "But don't do anything too sudden, or Mr. Colt here will start coughing."

"My name's Slocum," he said. "John Slocum."

"All right, Mr. Slocum," Chino said nastily, pulling up on the other side of him. "Lead the way."

Slocum glanced quickly around and saw at least fourteen, maybe fifteen riders at his back. A small army. The trail boss had not been bluffing. He had left Oregon determined either to bring that herd through safely or to find and hang the rustlers who had been stripping him and the other Oregon drovers. Slocum wondered how long this nasty business had been brewing. From the look of things, it had been going on for a long, bitter time.

Clapping spurs to his mount, Slocum led the way out of the timber and out onto the parkland, following the hoofmarks left by the charging cattle, his mind racing well ahead of them. Somehow, in some way, he would have to break loose of this small army. And all he could do was keep them moving until that moment arrived.

Keep them moving, and act like he knew where he was taking them.

3

Slocum's opportunity came at mid-day when the trail boss decided to camp by a mountain stream to rest and water the horses.

Slocum had ridden steadily at the head of the drovers with Chino on one side and the trail boss, Harry, on the other. He led them into a broad canyon, the hoofprints of the herd that had taken this route still fresh enough to follow without dismounting. As he rode, Slocum had been careful to keep his gaze casual and to follow the trail he took without hesitation. It would not be wise, he realized, to look the least bit uncertain. These men had to be convinced that he had taken this route before—that it was all quite familiar to him.

Now, as he sat back cross-legged against a tree trunk and sipped from his canteen, he stole a glance at his mount. After watering the pony, he had pretended to loosen the cinch. Instead, he had tightened it. He had let the pony's reins fall loosely over a branch, though he had been at some pains to give the impression that he had tied the horse securely to it.

The stream was shallow, not more than ten yards away, and less than a couple of yards wide. Beyond it was the entrance to a narrow, steep-sided canyon. On the far side of the canyon was a wilderness of boulders and scrub pine. Once he reached the shelter of those boulders, he reckoned, he would be safe. The trick was to mount his horse quickly enough to be able to make it across the stream and into that canyon before any of his captors could get off an accurate shot.

But first things first. He had to get rid of Chino.

Chino was sticking close to Slocum, and it was obvious why: he was hoping Slocum would make a break so he could ventilate him. For some reason, Chino did not trust Slocum, and had been continually mocking him all that morning as he rode beside him.

It was almost as if he knew Slocum was just buying time.

At the moment Chino was on his feet beside Slocum, his back resting against a pine, a tin cup of water in his hand. Stirring restlessly, he straightened up and threw what water he had left onto the ground.

"Hey, Harry!" he called.

The trail boss was near the stream, talking to a drover hunkered down beside him. Glancing back, he frowned. "What do you want, Chino?"

"How much longer we going to follow this son of a bitch?" Chino demanded.

"Why you askin'?"

"Because I don't think he knows where he's goin' any more than I do."

"He's doin' fine, for Christ's sake. Lay off him, will you?" As he spoke, Harry got to his feet and looked with some irritation at Chino. "Don't you want to find these bastards? What the hell are you after, anyway?"

"Damn it, Harry! Him and his men killed three of ours. I don't trust him. He's just waiting for a chance to break loose from us. He ain't gonna take us to that ranch."

"So you want his blood, is that it? A chance to stretch his neck. And I bet you'll be the one to give his horse a slap."

"Sure. Why not?"

Harry took a step closer to Chino. "How come you're so bloodthirsty all of a sudden?"

Pushing himself away from the tree, Chino took a step closer to the trail boss. "Hell, Harry! That ain't fair, you sayin' that. Pete Coslow and Will are dead because of him. All I want is justice."

The moment Chino's back was to him, Slocum vaulted to his feet. Slamming his canteen down onto Chino's head, he leaped onto his pony's back. Before a shot was fired, Slocum had snatched up the pony's reins and clapped his spurs to its flanks. He bowled through the startled cowpunchers and rode across the stream. Ducking into the canyon, he galloped along the near wall until he reached another stream. Putting the pony across it, he rode hard for the boulders on the far side. Gunshots echoed off the vaulting walls and a round ricocheted off the face of a boulder just ahead of him. He did not look back. A moment later he had ridden deep inside the tangle of boulders.

Behind him, the canyon echoed with the sudden clatter of hooves as the drovers galloped into the canyon after him. By this time, Slocum had ridden deep into the pines beyond the boulders, following a narrow game trail that led to a ridge above him. The trail was steep and treacherous, the pine needles slippery under his pony's hooves, but the sure-footed animal slipped only twice, recovering nicely both times.

As soon as he reached the ridge safely, Slocum flung himself from his saddle, ripped open his bedroll, and fished out his remaining Colt. Peering over the lip of the ridge, he saw the horsemen entering the pines. The floor of the woodland, covered as it was with a heavy blanket of needles, left no sign of his passage. The drovers charged on through the pines and down the canyon without a single glance to right or left. Waiting until the sound of their passage had died completely, Slocum stood up, holstered his gun, and mounted.

The canyon's rim loomed high above him. The trail winding up toward it looked even more treacherous than the one he had just negotiated. But Slocum craved height as well as distance. Those riders would double back soon enough and, when they returned, Slocum wanted to be as high above them as he could get.

He turned his pony about and started for the rim. He was better than three quarters of the way to it when he was forced to dismount and lead the pony. Twice Slocum had to dig his heels in and hang on as the pony lost its footing and began to slide back down the talus-littered slope. But the pony seemed to realize that he could count on Slocum's judgment and never became unmanageable.

It was at least two hours after he started the climb before Slocum scrambled up onto the canyon rim, pulling the pony up onto it after him. Exhausted, Slocum let the pony crop the sparse grass at his feet. For a while he thought he could hear the distant rumble of riders in one of the many canyons below him. But soon there was nothing but the silence of the high country, puncutated by the occasional song of a robin and the chitter of chipmunks.

Idly, he glanced to his right, at a mountain in the distance that loomed still higher into the cold spring sky. At once he found himself remembering what one of the rustlers had called out:

I'll ride on to Horse Peak and meet you there. Tell Slade.

The mountain Slocum was gazing at resembled with startling fidelity the head of a horse.

Horse Peak!

Scrambling to his feet, he mounted up. This was no time to rest. Though the peak was some distance away, if he got there soon enough there was a chance he might meet up once again with Slade and that ferret-faced sidekick of his.

For the first few miles, Slocum was forced to keep to the canyon rim, and as he followed its winding course he watched Horse Peak slowly change in appearance as a different face was gradually presented to Slocum's gaze. Before Slocum camped for the night, the peak no longer resembled a horse's head from the new angle. Slocum had been lucky—very lucky—to have glanced up and seen the peak when he did.

He started up again at daybreak, and as he rode through that long day, he saw how easily a herd—or a hundred herds, for that matter—could be funnelled through this torturous, canyon-riddled land. Spending another night camped under the stars, he got up early the next morning, shot an unwary rabbit, and ate heartily, swilling the meat down with coffee. He wished he had grain for his mount, but the pony seemed content enough with the graze he found nearby.

By mid-afternoon of the third day, Slocum became aware of a great barrier rim lifting into the sky on the other side of Horse Peak. What lay beyond that rim, Slocum could only guess. Perhaps still another land of rugged peaks and canyons.

It was close to sundown when Slocum reached Horse Peak. He was still quite high, the barrier rim now appearing before him as a series of steep, dark hills shouldering close by towering, jagged peaks. He cut down through a tangle of boulders and scrub pine, heading for the timberline below him.

Breaking out of the timber at last, he cantered across the valley floor toward a broad stream that cut along the base of the mountain. Splashing across the stream, he came upon dormant camp fires that had burned themselves out no more than a day before.

Dismounting, Slocum watered his horse, then drank deeply himself. As he straightened up and looked about him, he saw the unmistakable signs of milling animals almost everywhere his eyes rested. On both sides of the stream the ground was torn up and the banks ravaged. Though the stream was a swift one flowing over gravel, it was still cloudy with mud from the loosened bank.

There was no doubt that this was where the stolen herd had regrouped before moving on. And Slocum was only a day or so behind it. He decided to make his camp in the pines that night and take up the trail at daybreak.

By mid-morning of the next day Slocum had followed the herd's trail beyond Horse Peak into the barrier rim and found himself once more in the midst of a hard, vaulting land that towered above him on all sides. The trail led around the shoulders of mountains that blanketed distance with their vast bulk. Soon he found himself close by white fields of snow, a gaunt land where only a few warped and stunted conifers clung to tiny footholds between the rocks.

Cutting winds swept along every canyon, slicing at Slocum relentlessly. By noon he was lost in this tumbling upland labyrinth of rock and great slashed canyons that twisted and fell, then angled and tumbled back before the wall of peaks. Slocum had only the trail left by the herd to guide him: the pulverized rock, the tufts of hair wedged in the cracks of the walls against which the hazed cattle had milled as they were pushed on. Once, where the shale-littered trail threaded along the rim of a deep canyon, Slocum saw far below the bloated carcasses of at least three steers, some already picked clean by vultures.

By mid-afternoon he was following the trail across a high, tight valley. When night came, he picked a sheltered *rincón* off the trail and camped there. He still had no grain for his pony and he had not sighted anything he could shoot for himself to eat. He watered the pony, rubbed it down, then rolled up in his slicker under a shelf of rock to sleep.

He was beginning to feel somewhat discouraged the next morning as, stiff and sore, cold and hungry, he set out once again. It was a gray, sunless morning, and a raw wind that smelled of rain beat against his face. It seemed to him as he traveled between these rugged peaks that he might well be doomed to ride endlessly, without ever leaving these vast, towering mountains shrouded in thunderheads. Still, he kept on doggedly, and by noon he could tell he was traveling a decided downslope, and had been for hours.

Soon he saw thin timber opening up below the trail, then heavier timber and brush. Finally he was free of the cold mountain walls. Through a gap in the shrouded mountains he glimpsed a dark, wide valley. It was green below, the cold green of pines and junipers.

Down through this timber the dim trail of the rustled herd took him until it petered out at last amidst a tumble of foothills. The herd had reached its destination and was splitting up once again. Slocum kept going. On the valley floor, he picked up a wet, rutted road and continued on deeper into the valley, past the forbidding mountains that hemmed it in on either side. Toward nightfall, when the valley narrowed, he saw ahead of him in the distance a bleak town, made up for the most part of board and log shacks, with only a few false-fronted buildings to give the place any substance. Though the clouds had cleared somewhat, above the town the heavy mist had dissolved into a thin rain.

Reaching the town, Slocum worked his way down the single muddy street to the feed stable where he gave his weary pony to a boy for graining. Looking about him, Slocum saw the place was almost barren of women. Men clustered in surly groups in front of saloons and stores watched him closely, their eyes narrow, their hips overladen with gleaming hardware. As Slocum proceeded on foot farther down the street, not a single townsman greeted him or even nodded, but he could feel their eyes boring into him as he passed.

Slocum paused at last under a wooden awning that protected the customers of what appeared to be the town's fanciest watering hole, the Horse Head Saloon.

He pushed through the batwings and bellied up to the bar. He ordered a beer and took it over to a table in the corner. A quiet game of poker was in progress at a rear table and two very serious drinkers were nursing their whiskeys farther down the bar. That was about all the business in the place. Slocum nudged his hat back off his forehead and tipped his chair back, sipping his beer idly. It felt good to have something solid under his rump for a change.

Now all he had to do was find Slade—and that pleasant sidekick of his, Jimmy.

A woman came from the back, saw him sitting alone, and walked over to his table. She was in her early thirties and her lips and cheeks were heavily rouged. She wore her rust-colored hair down to her shoulders. Her long green dress accentuated her full bust and narrow waist. The best thing about her was her eyes. They were slanted slightly and were a deep emerald color.

"Do you like to drink alone, mister?" she asked.

"I hate it," Slocum said. "Sit down."

She sat, motioned to the barkeep for a drink, then turned to face Slocum. "My name is Jenny," she said. "I own this place."

"How's business?"

"It'll get much better tonight." The barkeep brought her a shot glass full of whiskey.

Slocum sipped his beer.

"What's your name?" Jenny asked.

"Slocum. John Slocum."

"You're new in town."

"I am pleased you noticed," he said with a smile.

"Where you from?"

"Do I have to tell you?"

She smiled. "Yes."

"Why?"

"It will be better if you do," she replied quite seriously.

"Two weeks ago I was in New Mexico. I found it a much warmer, more hospitable place than this high country of yours."

SLOCUM AND THE CATTLE QUEEN 31

"There are those who like the high country." She smiled. "I am one."

"What's this place called?" Slocum asked.

"Coleman Flats."

He nodded and continued to sip his beer. It sure was flat.

"Are you a lawman?" Jenny asked.

"No. Are you looking for someone to tame this place?"

She smiled. "We have a sheriff. But I warn you—if you are a lawman, it would be better for you to tell me. I can see that you get out of here safely."

"*You* will see to it?" he asked, incredulous.

"Yes. I have influence with Sheriff Busher."

"Relax. I'm not a lawman."

"Then what are you doing in this valley?" she persisted.

"I am looking for a man called Slade and his sidekick. I have business with them. Unfinished business."

She frowned. "Slade Banner and Jimmy Bright?"

"Yes."

"Why don't you just go to the Lazy C?"

"Slade told me to meet him at the Horse Head."

She leaned back in her chair and regarded him closely for a long moment. "I warn you, if you are the law, you're in great danger in this town."

"I gathered that when I rode in here."

"Will you have another beer?"

Slocum shook his head and stood up. "I think I'll get some food into me first. And a room."

"There is a restaurant across the street."

"I noticed."

"But there is no hotel in Coleman Flats."

Slocum smiled. "I'll find a bed, Jenny."

She smiled too then. "Yes. I have no doubt you will. The few women left in this town hunger for new men. Good luck to you, John Slocum."

He thanked her, left the saloon, and crossed the street to the small restaurant. He ate heartily, then beckoned to the woman who had served him.

She was a slim, blonde girl who wore no rouge. She had watched him warily, almost fearfully, as he sat down and ordered. He had smiled and eaten cheerfully what she had set before him, and this had appeared to relax her somewhat; but she was still nervous.

"My name is John Slocum," he told her. "I am looking for a place to sleep tonight. Can you help me?"

"I have a room above the restaurant," she told him coldly. "I rent it out once in a while. It is not cheap."

"Neither am I," Slocum said, dropping a silver dollar onto the table. "How much for the night?"

"Five dollars."

Slocum's eyebrows shot up. "You must be *very* good."

She slapped him, then stepped back, terrified at what she had done.

"My apologies," he said to her. "That was an unkind remark. But your price is rather steep."

"I must live, too," she said, the color flowing

SLOCUM AND THE CATTLE QUEEN 33

back into her cheeks. "I—I am sorry I slapped you."

"Forget it. If the bed is as warm as your temper, I should sleep well."

"That will be five dollars in advance," she said.

He paid her and stood up. "Lead the way," he told her.

He followed her out through the kitchen, past a Chinese cook, and up a flight of outside wooden stairs. There were two rooms. One was the sitting room and contained a wood stove and a sofa. The other was the bedroom. On the bedroom door was a bolt that could be worked only from the sitting room.

"You may have the bedroom," she told him. "I will sleep in here."

"I don't like to be locked in."

"Then sleep elsewhere."

He shrugged. He was too exhausted to argue with the girl. He nodded and moved foggily into the bedroom. The beer and then the meal had made him groggy. He slumped down onto the bed and grinned sleepily out at the girl.

"What's your name?" he asked.

"Mandy. Mandy O'Brien."

"Well, Mandy, good night."

She closed the door. He waited for her to shoot the bolt, but all he heard was her light footsteps on the outside stairs as she returned to the restaurant. Turning, he glanced out the window, down at the town's main street. He was in time to see a lone rider, who looked like the kid who had taken his horse at the livery, gallop out from the alley behind the Horse Head Saloon and head north out of town.

Toward the Lazy C, Slocum had no doubt.

He worked quickly, before sleep could claim him. Removing the mattress from the spring, he dropped it to the floor behind the bed. Then he covered over the spring with the coverlet and bunched up both pillows to make it look as if he were sleeping in the bed.

Then he lay down on the mattress behind the bed, his Colt in his hand. The last thing he removed before he fell asleep was his hat. He was too exhausted to kick off his boots.

4

Slocum was awake instantly. It was Mandy who had entered the room. In the light from the sitting room, he watched her approach his bed and poke with some surprise at the empty bed above him.

From below the bed he said softly, "What's wrong, Mandy?"

She uttered a tiny, startled cry and jumped back. He eased himself up onto the bed, his .44 still in his hand. "Just a precaution," he told her. "Now what is it?"

"I came to warn you."

"About what?"

"I been hearing talk. The hostler has been sent after Slade Banner. And the sheriff wants to know all about you. This is a bad town, Mr. Slocum. You better get out."

"Thanks for warning me. I appreciate it. But I'm too tired to leave right now, and Slade Banner is just the man I want to see."

"You are a fool, then. I shouldn't have come up here to warn you. Go back to sleep."

"Not now," he said, reaching out gently and taking her by the hand. "It was kind of you to worry about me. I don't want you to think I'm ungrateful."

She did not try to pull away. Sitting down on the edge of the bed beside him, she said, "I'm sorry I slapped you. That was not nice."

"What I said was not nice."

Their closeness was causing her pale complexion to flush slightly. In the dim lantern light that filtered in from the sitting room, he saw tiny beads of perspiration on her upper lip. Her eyes had looked blue in the restaurant. They seemed darker now, almost purple.

"Are you a lawman?" she asked. "Is it Slade Banner you want?"

"I am not a lawman, but I do want to see Slade Banner."

"He's dangerous."

"I know."

Their voices had grown softer, more intimate. She leaned closer and turned her face up to his. He kissed her on the lips. They were moist and warm and opened hungrily to his probing tongue. In that instant Slocum realized how much he needed a woman.

"Get undressed," he told her, his voice husky.

Wordlessly, she stood up. As her fingers flew down her dress, unhooking the buttons from waist to hem, Slocum hauled the mattress back up onto the bedspring, kicked off his boots, and stepped out of his pants. She gasped when she saw the size of him. He did not know if it was with pleasurable anticipation or fear. She undid her corset and stepped out of her chemise. Sitting back down on the bed, her glance still resting on his erection, she loosened her long blonde hair. It fell almost past her waist. With one hand on her shoulder, Slocum gently turned her to face him, then pressed her down upon the mattress.

For a moment he feasted his eyes on her pale, almost shimmering nakedness. Slim though she was, her breasts were more than ample, her curves generously rounded. She opened her arms to him and spread her legs. He slipped into her effortlessly, the moist warmth of her closing about him like hot silk. His big, callused hands scooped up her buttocks and thrust her pelvis hungrily up toward him. She gasped and flung her arms still more tightly about his neck. Abruptly, Slocum held still. He did not dare to thrust. In his present state he would come almost immediately if he did not use all the skill he possessed to prolong his erection.

Deliberately, he bore down heavily upon her, impaling her on his rigid lance. With a delighted gasp, she began to build swiftly to her climax, her muscles squeezing him, milking him, her head tossing from side to side. At last, with a sudden cry of joy and pain and release, she came.

She came for a very long time, but still Slocum bore into her, his throbbing cock as hard as a bar of steel.

"Oh, you're still inside me! Still there!" she cried,

running her fingers through his hair and covering his face with kisses. "Oh, it feels so good!"

"Yes," he muttered, pulling her over until she was straddling him.

She gasped as she sank still further onto his shaft. Reaching up, he stroked her breasts, slow and gentle, circling her nipples with his thumbs, around and around. She leaned back and closed her eyes, moaning softly. Then he slipped his hands caressingly down to her hips and thighs.

Her long blonde tresses swung forward. He looked up through her hair at her glassy eyes and parted mouth. She licked her lips drowsily, her breath catching in her throat. Slowly she began to rock back and forth. She was no longer breathing now—she was panting like a she-cougar as her hips began to move in slow, steady thrusts, back and forth, like a rider easing a horse along at a walk.

As she kept that pace, he began to run his hands over her body, down her back to the outside of her thighs where they straddled him. He was doing what he could to keep his mind off that searing pole buried deep within her, but the urgent scream in his loins was building with each passing second as she rocked above him, his cock still primed, still unfired. He could hold off no longer.

"Now," he told her. "Ride, woman! Ride!"

"Yes," she hissed. "Yes!"

Thrusting forward and down, her hips broke into a wild, rapid, lunging rhythm. He was astonished at how deep he plowed. Her eyes shut, her face a tight mask of pleasure, she made a sound deep within her throat, wild and not quite human. She began uttering tiny, sharp little barks of pleasure. He rose up to meet her thrusts, abandoning himself at last, catching her hips in his big hands to keep her on him. Panting wildly with each thrust, she leaned forward over him. The nipples of her bobbing breasts flicked at his face.

Reaching up, he rolled her over swiftly, and with a powerful, reckless lunge, drove deep down into her, aware of nothing now but his own frantic, building tension. He thought he could hear himself laughing as a sharp, exquisite pain seared his loins. He exploded, filling her to the brim and riveting her to the bed beneath him. Clinging to her with each pulsing ejaculation, he burrowed still deeper into her.

Drunk with the delight of it, he was only dimly aware of her own soaring, keening cry of pleasure, of her legs swinging up to enclose his waist, her arms grappling his neck. So tightly did she cleave to him that he found himself gasping for breath.

They pulled apart, laughing. Flushed, perspiration pouring off them both, still laughing like kids after a long race, they lay side by side on the bed. A delicious sense of fullness stole over Slocum.

He kissed her on the nose at last and said, "Thank you for waking me up. It *was* to warn me, wasn't it?"

"Yes," she said, laughing. "That too."

"Well, thank you."

"It was my pleasure," she replied.

She kissed him on the lips, slipped from the bed, and, gathering up her clothes, moved out of the bedroom. She did not slide the bolt after she closed the door.

Heavy with sleep, Slocum again pulled the mattress onto the floor, fashioned the two pillows into a reasonable facsimile of himself, and lay back down on the mattress under the bed. With his hand once more clasped about the grip of the Colt, he slept, this time with a faint, satiated smile on his face.

The young hostler Jenny had sent galloping out of town that night had been given a message to be delivered to Slade Banner. But the hostler was not heading for the Lazy C. As Jenny Warren well new, Slade was still in the hills north of town, cutting out and branding the stock he would be keeping for the Lazy C.

The hostler's name was Tim. He was a slim, bony towhead of sixteen. He wasn't sure himself where he had gotten the name he now answered to, but he no longer questioned it. Following the directions Miss Jenny had given him, he made good time. In less than an hour he cantered into a wide canyon, at the far end of which he saw winking camp fires. As he rode closer he heard the bawling of unhappy cattle and frightened, motherless calves. Figures materialized out of the darkness as they passed before the branding fires. As he dismounted a moment later, he was surrounded by the grim Lazy C riders.

"Where's Slade?" Tim asked.

Slade materialized out of the darkness, a glowing branding iron in his hand.

"I got a message for you," Tim said, striding toward him.

Slade flung the branding iron to the ground and looked at the note Tim held out to him. "Read it to me," he said to the boy.

Opening it, Tim crouched over a branding fire and read the message aloud. Then Slade took it, crumpled the note, dropped it into the fire, and looked quickly around. By this time all branding had come to a halt and a crowd had gathered around Tim and Slade.

"Jimmy!" Slade called.

Jimmy Bright pushed through the ranks of weary punchers. Beads of perspiration were rolling down his grimy face. "What do you want?" he asked.

"Slocum," Slade told him. "John Slocum. You remember him?"

"Sure I remember him."

"You took care of him."

Jimmy Bright shifted his feet impatiently. "What's this all about, Slade?"

"John Slocum is in Coleman Flats."

Jimmy Bright peered intently and incredulously at Slade for a moment. Then he looked around to see if this was some sort of joke. "Slocum?" he asked.

"That's right, Jimmy—the marshal you was supposed to have killed."

"He's in town?"

"Yes, damn it!"

"Hell, I saw the son of a bitch go down in the middle of that stampede. Them cattle was all over him. It *couldn't* be Slocum."

"I just got a note from Jenny. A big, curious gent named John Slocum was inquiring about us in the Horse Head. You think there could be two John Slocums looking for this herd?"

Jimmy turned to Tim. "You seen this gent?"

Tim nodded. "I grained his mount."

"Describe him."

"A big man, better than six foot, I'd say. All shoulders. Moves quick. Got hair as black as a raven and green eyes."

"What's he riding?" Jimmy asked.

"A spotted pony," the boy replied.

"Jesus," Jimmy said softly. "That's him all right."

"Go back down there and finish him," Slade said to Jimmy. "And do it tonight. Get Busher to help."

"I don't need that fool sheriff's help."

"Just get the son of a bitch. I don't know how he did it, but he was able to trail us all the way here. He must be part Indian, to track us through them mountains. Make sure he ain't got anyone with him. Then kill him."

Jimmy Bright's mouth a thin line of resolve, he nodded. "I'll get my horse, Tim," he told the hostler. "Ride back with you."

Tim nodded and mounted up. As he sat his horse to wait for Jimmy Bright, Slade moved closer and peered up at him. "You seen a lot tonight, Tim. I guess Jenny trusts you."

Tim swallowed and nodded.

"Just you be sure you can be trusted. Hear, Tim?"

"Sure, Slade."

Slade stepped back from the horse. Jimmy Bright

rode up then, nodded to Tim, and moved out ahead of him back up the canyon. In a moment the two horsemen had vanished into the darkness.

Slade turned to the others. "Get them branding irons hot!" he called out. "We ain't through yet!"

As the men scurried back to the fires, Slade frowned and stared into the night after the two riders. This Slocum was sure as hell a lot tougher than he or Jimmy Bright had realized. And Slade was not so sure Jimmy was going to be able to take care of the son of a bitch this time, either.

Slocum was trouble.

But who the hell was he?

Mel Floren hurried over to him. "We got more company, Slade," he said, pointing to the north.

Slade looked in the direction Mel was pointing and saw five riders moving across the moonlit parkland, scattering cattle as they rode. He recognized the lead rider at once from the black felt derby he favored. It was H.C. Benson. He was not due until that morning, but he had come early, Slade had no doubt, to make sure he got all he could. The four other riders with him were his drovers.

Slade walked slowly toward the riders until they were close enough to greet him. They pulled up and remained in the saddle as Benson dismounted and hurried over to him, a broad smile on his face. He was a big, powerful man dressed in a dark woolen suit, with a silver watch chain looped across his silken vest. His powerful, thrusting jaw was clean-shaven, his eyebrows beetling, the eyes under them shifting and quick.

"We been cutting through some herd," he told Slade, pleased. "This sure as hell beats that last one you brought in."

"It's a big one, all right," Slade Banner agreed.

Benson rubbed his hands together happily. "Hell, if you ain't greedy, Slade, it'll leave me enough for two agency contracts."

"We still talking the same price?"

"A deal's a deal, Slade," Benson said, slapping his partner on the back. "Yes, sir, a deal's a deal."

"You got that much with you?"

"I wasn't expecting you to bring in this many head."

Slade smiled. "Neither was I. I'll have to keep most of this new maverick stock in the benchlands and feed them into the lowland herds real slow, like. I don't want Maria asking too many questions."

Benson grinned. "She still willing to believe these are just mavericks?"

"She wants to build her ranch, make it as big as the one she and her father had in Texas. It's very important to her. Maybe she knows, maybe she doesn't want to know. Meanwhile, I'll just let her think what a fine ramrod I am, and what nutritious grasses we got on the Lazy C range."

Benson laughed. "How soon can we move out the culls?"

"By mid-morning." Slade indicated the four drovers with Benson. "If those four hands you brought with you can pitch in, maybe sooner."

"I'll see to it."

"About what you owe me—there's at least five hundred head more than you bargained for."

"I will give you my IOU, and I'll deliver on it in Coleman Flats in two weeks."

"Done," said Slade and the two shook hands.

Benson left him then to direct his drovers to help in the branding of the beef Slade was selecting for Maria Coleman's Lazy C. As Slade knew, once on the other side of the mountains, Benson had a full crew waiting to alter the brands on the culls Slade left him.

It was a good deal all around. For four years now they had been in partnership, Slade plundering the herds being shipped over the mountains from Oregon, then selecting the best stock for the Lazy C and selling the rest to Benson to fulfill the cattle dealer's government contracts for the Indian agencies.

Moving back to help out in the branding, Slade took a deep breath. So far this had been his best haul. Come next fall, he would be in a position to push for full partnership in the Lazy C as Maria Coleman's husband. Her father had been dead for five years now, and it was time she took herself a husband. That such a woman had not already done so was a real shame. To think of all that going to waste kept Slade awake nights.

He did not see how she could refuse his offer. They got along well enough, and Slade had been careful never to push his attentions on her. And there was no doubt she admired him for the way his management of the ranch had steadily raised the quality of Lazy C beef. Right now the Lazy C was the most prosperous ranch in the valley, and Maria knew it.

So Jimmy had better take care of this Slocum. Slade was too close to his goal now to have it ruined by some damned federal marshal.

Slocum lifted his head from the mattress and closed his right hand tightly about the grip of his .44. He could tell from the stealthy way in which the door swung open that this visitor wasn't Mandy.

In that fleeting instant, he wished he still had his old .36 caliber Navy Colt. It had a faster first shot than the .44 Peacemaker he now held in his hand. But as the small, wiry figure of Jimmy Bright stepped crouching through the open doorway, Slocum decided it was no time to quibble.

Jimmy's right fist was big with a revolver. Watching from the floor at the foot of the bed, Slocum waited. He needed to know if Jimmy had anyone with him. Mandy had mentioned something about the sheriff. Apparently, however, Jimmy Bright was alone. With no hesitation at all, he thrust out his weapon and fired four rounds into the pillows Slocum had put on the bed. Not satisfied, Jimmy moved still closer. This time, aiming at what he perceived to be Slocum's resting head, he emptied his .44.

In such a small room, the six reports sounded like detonations. The walls reverberated and the floor heaved. The air was heavy with the acrid stench of black powder smoke. Deliberately, without any wasted motion, Slocum grasped the frame of the bed and levered his body into position. Like a rattler striking from a crevice, he fired point-blank into Jimmy Bright's chest. Slocum heard the satisfying thunk of lead striking flesh, as the little man slammed back against the wall.

Dropping his gun, he cried, "Don't kill me, Slocum! My gun's empty!"

"All right," Slocum said.

He pulled himself erect and watched as Jimmy Bright slid crookedly down the wall to the floor, his head lolling.

Walking across the room to inspect his would-be killer, Slocum heard the pound of footsteps on stairs and then the outside door was flung open. A beefy, round-bellied brute of a man charged past the sitting room and into the bedroom. He was holding a Smith and Wesson in his right hand.

Slocum spun to cover him. At once the big man pulled up and hastily lowered his gun. A tin star was pinned to his greasy vest.

"You'd be the sheriff," Slocum said.

"And who in hell are you?"

"The man Jimmy Bright came up here to kill. John Slocum. You didn't know anything about it, I suppose."

"Of course not."

The sheriff bent to inspect the wounded man. He gasped and looked up at Slocum.

"You've killed him!" he cried. "Jimmy Bright's dead!"

A groan came from the sitting room. Slocum strode past the sheriff and found Mandy O'Brien sitting up on her sofa, rubbing her head gingerly. He could tell from the look on her face that she was in pain.

"What's the matter?" he asked her.

She blinked uncertainly up at him and continued to rub her head. "My head. It hurts!"

He felt her head gently. There was a large lump on the top of her head along the side. Jimmy Bright must have clubbed her before opening the door to the inner room.

"Did you bolt my door?" he asked her.

She shook her head.

He knew she had not. If the door had been bolted, Jimmy Bright would have simply thrown the bolt and stormed in, firing. Finding the door unlocked, he had decided to enter quietly and kill Slocum in his sleep.

Slocum felt the sheriff's gun barrel shoved into his back. It was not a gentle poke.

"You're under arrest, Slocum," the sheriff told him. "Hand me that gun, butt first."

Slocum turned and did as he was told. "What's the charge?" he asked.

"Murder. The murder of Jimmy Bright."

"Hell, he came up here to kill me. It was self-defense."

The sheriff smiled coldly. "All right, then. I'm locking you up for discharging a firearm within the town limits."

"Is that all?"

"And disturbing the peace," the sheriff went on.

"What about hunting without a license, you son of a bitch?"

The sheriff stuck Slocum's .44 into his own belt. "Turn around and march."

"Where to?"

"We got a lockup down the street. Head for it."

Glancing down at Mandy, Slocum asked, "Are you going to be all right?"

Rubbing her head gingerly, she nodded. Her eyes were filled with concern for him.

Slocum patted her reassuringly on the shoulder and marched from the place. On the landing, he paused.

The sheriff bumped into him, the six-gun in his hand ramming Slocum hard.

"Damn it, Sheriff!" Slocum cried. "You don't need to stick that gun barrel clean through to the other side, do you?" Slocum half turned as he spoke.

The sheriff frowned and pulled the weapon back slightly. "Just keep on going down those steps, Slocum," he ordered.

But Slocum kept on turning. His left elbow swung down and knocked the sheriff's revolver aside. His right fist came around at the same time. With brutal effectiveness, he swung up hard, driving his fist deep into Busher's soft gut. The man gasped and sagged forward, his eyes bulging out of his head. For a moment Slocum thought he was going to cry. The sheriff dropped his weapon and Slocum heard it clatter down the steps. Reaching up with his left hand, Slocum grabbed Busher around the back of the neck, stepped aside, and hurled the big man past him down the stairway.

The sheriff landed head first, then tumbled clumsily,

ass over teakettle, muffled groans escaping him as he went. When he reached the ground, he was no longer groaning. Slocum raced down the stairs after him, retrieved his .44, and stuck the sheriff's gun into his own belt. A quick inspection of the unconscious lawman showed him to be breathing in sharp, spasmodic gasps. He had probably suffered a few broken ribs.

Slocum hurried back up to Mandy's room for his gear. Staying around this town was not at all healthy. Perhaps he would have better luck at the Lazy C, confronting Slade Banner openly.

It sure as hell couldn't be any worse.

5

Maria Coleman was tall, almost five feet ten, yet she weighed only a hundred and twenty pounds. A grown man could easily span her waist with his two hands, though no man had done so as yet. Her hair was as black as a raven's wing, her cheekbones sharp, almost gaunt, her neck long and graceful. But it was the shimmering gleam of her large, dark, almond-shaped eyes that caused men to halt in their work whenever she rode by.

At the moment she was high on a ridge, sitting astride her favorite black, a stallion only she could ride. She was wearing a broad-brimmed sombrero, a men's black, tight-fitting trousers, exquisite hand-tooled riding boots, a black vest trimmed in gold thread, and a white broadcloth man's shirt with a white silk bandanna knotted at her throat.

What she saw below her made her very angry, but she sat her horse quietly and continued to watch.

Maria had been almost seventeen when her father

had died, leaving her in the care of Antonio Carvalho, her father's faithful Mexican retainer, and the old Shoshone housekeeper and cook her father had slept with at the last. She had let Slade Banner and Antonio run the ranch for her in the years since, content to concentrate her attention almost entirely on the large, fast horses she bred in preference to the smaller mustangs and Indian ponies that abounded in the region. Over the extensive parklands of her range, she rode these magnificent animals like a man with a devil at his back, alarming Antonio and all those who saw her with her reckless, single-minded intensity.

But it was a long time now since the death of her father, and she was a twenty-one-year-old woman. This spring she had decided it was time for her to take a more active role in the running of her ranch. To begin with, she wanted to accompany Slade Banner when he took the Lazy C hands into the surrounding foothills and rounded up her stock. But before she had been able to make this wish of hers known to him, Slade had already left with most of the hands.

Annoyed, she had asked Antonio where Slade had gone to begin the roundup. At first Antonio had said he was not sure. Only when she persisted had Antonio reluctantly directed her into the mountains ringing her ranch to the south. But there she had found no trace of Slade or any of the men he had taken with him. She had ridden deep into the western reaches of her range. In her determined search, she rode high above the timberline, high enough eventually to skirt the still-deep snowfields. She found Lazy C cattle everywhere, and most of them had lasted through the winter in reasonably good shape, she was pleased to note. But no sign at all did she find of Slade or any other Lazy C rider.

She spent the next few days camping out under the stars and rounding up small gathers, which she hazed down to the valley's fresh, spring-fed pastures. Returning to the ranch, she again pressed Antonio for information about her foreman's whereabouts. This time her questions were more insistent, and at once she saw how this change in her attitude alarmed Antonio. Pulling back then, she had waited watchfully. Sure enough, the night before, a little after midnight, Antonio had ridden off, heading north.

Maria had followed.

It was full daylight now as Maria looked down upon Lazy C riders and watched them haze long files of cattle ahead of them into the draws and arroyos high above the valley floor. It was obvious that this was where Slade intended these cattle to remain until it was safe for them to be brought down into the valley with the rest of the Lazy C's stock. Even from this distance, she could see their raw, freshly singed hides where the brands had been altered. In some cases the running iron had done a clumsy job at best. The men must have worked throughout the night.

Meanwhile Antonio had located Slade and she could see the two of them astride their horses, talking close by a canyon wall. Maria was sure they were discussing the fact that she suspected something. But by now Maria no longer suspected. She knew. Slade Banner, the foreman of the Lazy C, was a cattle rustler.

A few minutes earlier, she had watched five men drive off a fairly large herd, heading southeast. Slade had shaken one of the men's hands before the herd pulled out. The fellow was wearing a derby. It was obvious to Maria that with the delivery of this herd to the buyer a deal had been consummated. Though Slade might have held back the best of the rustled stock for the Lazy C, he had sold the remainder. And what could be more natural than that? Maria thought bitterly. Why should Slade Banner be above lining his own pockets?

Though Maria remained outwardly calm as she sat her black, inwardly she was seething. For the first time she realized why the Lazy C stock prospered to the extent it had, and why Slade and the burgeoning prosperity of her ranch had seemed to arouse such bitter enmity from every other rancher in the area.

A fly lit upon her black's ear. The big, high-strung animal snorted angrily as he shook his powerful head. The sudden movement appeared to catch the attention of one of the drovers below. Swiftly, Maria drew back from the ridge, turned her mount, and began a fast canter back the way she had come.

She needed time to swallow her fury and gain some measure of control over her racing, tumultuous thoughts. Only too well did she realize that her future and that of the Lazy C depended on it.

* * *

Slade leaned back in his saddle and chuckled. "Of course Maria suspects something," he told Antonio. "What do you expect? She's a big girl now. She would have noticed sooner if she wasn't so wrapped up in them racehorses of hers. It's about time she began asking questions. Go on back to the ranch and let me tell her in my own way. Hell, she'll see things our way. We've given her a cattle kingdom the equal of the one her father left behind in Texas."

Antonio nodded wearily. The length of his mournful face was accentuated by his neatly trimmed little beard as snow-white as his hair. His eyes were large, brown liquid pools of sorrow and foreboding. "But we have done it with stolen cattle," he said to Slade.

"Name a rancher who hasn't helped himself along with a few mavericks now and then."

"A few, yes. But, Señor Banner, you have turned entire herds into mavericks."

"You knew all about it, Antonio. Are you getting cold feet now?" Slade demanded.

"It is just that I do not know what Maria will think when she finds out."

Slade grinned at the unhappy man, his dark eyes dancing. "I have seen her ride those horses of hers. She likes to move fast, Antonio. All I have done is speed things up a bit. She will not protest once she sees what we have built up for her as a result."

"Señor Banner, she is a woman. She is headstrong, like her father. How can we predict what she will think? It is not possible for us to do so, I am afraid."

Mel Floren rode over to them and pulled up respectfully some distance away to preserve their privacy. But it was apparent to Slade that the young redhead was worried about something.

Turning to him, Slade asked, "What is it, Mel?"

"I think I saw a rider up there." He indicated the ridge to their right with a quick nod.

Slade glanced up but saw nothing. "When?" he asked.

"A few minutes ago."

"You sure of this?"

Mel nodded.

"Did you get a good look?"

"Yes, I did, Slade. It was a woman astride a black."

Antonio swore softly.

Slade took a deep breath. The fat was in the fire. "You think it was Maria?" he asked Mel.

"At that distance I couldn't be absolutely sure. Whoever it was vanished pretty damn quick."

"But it could have been."

"Yes."

"All right, Mel."

Pursing his lips thoughtfully, Slade watched Mel ride back to the others. He patted his own horse's neck and glanced wearily back at Antonio. "Maria followed you," he said to the old Mexican.

"Yes."

"Stay here with the men. I think I'm going to have to go after her and explain things right now."

With an unhappy nod, Antonio pulled his horse back, then rode after Mel Floren. He rode ramrod-straight in his saddle, his right arm hanging down past his thigh—an old, meddling retainer Slade should have taken care of long before.

Though he had not wanted to alarm Antonio, Slade was more than a little worried about Maria's reaction when she learned the truth. She was certainly as intelligent as her father and easily as headstrong. That she had had the gumption to follow Antonio last night proved this conclusively.

He clapped spurs to his mount and lifted his horse to a quick gallop on a course that would take him out through the draw and up onto that ridge. He was hoping he would be able to overtake Maria before she got back to the ranch.

Maria was within sight of the Lazy C when Slade's shout alerted her. Glancing back over her shoulder, she saw her foreman topping a rise. Frowning angrily, she pulled up and turned her horse about to wait for Slade to reach her.

"You were back there in the hills," Slade said, yanking his mount to a halt beside her. "You saw the cattle."

"You mean the rustled cattle."

"Yes," Slade admitted, shoving his hat back off his forehead. "But it sounds better if you call them mavericks."

"Mavericks are unclaimed, unbranded cattle. I saw where the brands on these cattle had been altered. It is just as well you overtook me. I can tell you now, Slade—you're fired. And so is every one of the men who rode with you this past week."

"Simmer down, Maria. It's not as simple as that."

She looked at him for a long moment, her expression cold, her dark eyes gleaming. "Go on," she said. "Tell me what you mean by that."

Slade crossed his arms and regarded her coolly. She saw the grudging respect in his eyes and realized he was sorry this moment had come. But she had no doubt that, long before this, Slade Banner had prepared himself for it.

"I am not going to let you stop me now, Maria. I can't. I have spent four years building up the Lazy C. You can't expect me to walk away from all this now."

"You are a thief and God knows what else. You are not going to walk away from all this. You are going to run. Now."

"No, Maria. I told you. I can't—and I won't."

"You will leave this ranch today," she repeated firmly.

"It is not your decision to make."

"This is *my* ranch!"

"Stocked with cattle me and my men risked our lives gathering."

This casual defiance stopped her momentarily. "Then you will not do as I say?"

He smiled coldly. "No."

"Then I will get the law."

He laughed softly. "You will not get much help from Sheriff Busher."

"You own him too, do you?"

" 'Fraid so, Maria."

"There's Milt Gulick of The Bench. Sam Neuberger of the Bar N. And there are other ranchers. Soon this whole valley will know what I know," Maria said.

"If you do that, Maria, I will ruin you."

For the first time Maria was afraid. She felt her cheeks flaming angrily. "You would threaten a woman—a girl you helped bring up."

Slade nodded grimly. "More than that, Maria, I'll burn you out. The big main house first, of course. Then the barns and all those big, fine horses you love to ride. Who knows? You might get caught in the flames trying to save them. And when the smoke clears, your cattle will be gone—halfway to market by that time." His smile grew even colder. "And with no one the wiser, no one to mourn the passing of Maria Coleman."

"You son of a bitch," she hissed. "May you fry in hell!"

"Good. That sounds like you know who you are dealing with now. I suggest you do not forget it, Maria. The Lazy C is the finest spread in this county, and you are on your way to becoming the most powerful cattlewoman in the state. Instead of trying to cancel out what I have done to make the Lazy C what it is today, maybe you should count your blessings."

"Count my blessings! I have been sleeping with scorpions!"

As she spoke, she snatched up her riding crop and slashed the foreman across the cheek. Slade recoiled and ducked low. Furious, Maria continued to flail at him. After two more mean cracks about the face, Slade's composure broke. With an angry snarl, he twisted the riding crop out of her hand and flung it away.

Maria wheeled her black and started to gallop away, but Slade's blood was up by this time. He spurred after her, overtook her mount, and, reaching down, grabbed the horse's bridle. Yanking back cruelly, he sent the horse twisting to the turf. With a tiny, startled cry Maria went flying over its head. Dismounting, Slade grabbed Maria brutally by the hair and hauled her to her feet.

She began beating his chest, but it only seemed to increase his strength. His fist in her hair, he bent her face back, then stepped close to her, thrusting his body against hers. Rage and lust blazed from his eyes as he chuckled meanly down at her. Crying out, Maria managed to reach out with her hooked fingers, raking the side of his face. He flung her to the ground and drew his revolver.

She knew at once that he intended to kill her. He had no choice, since there could be little doubt in his mind that she would not go along with his filthy schemes. Scrambling to her feet, she started to run. But Slade was too quick. He grabbed her by the shoulder, spun her around, then clubbed her brutally on the side of the head.

As the universe exploded deep within her skull, Maria crumpled to the ground. Slade's face loomed close. It was a mean, twisted mask of hate. She saw him raise his gun. The muzzle of the Colt stared down at her like the mouth of a cannon.

A moment before she lost consciousness, she thought she heard a distant gunshot.

6

Slocum had reined in his pony when he saw the two figures on the slope below him. The moment he saw the girl begin to strike out at Slade Banner with her riding crop, he put his horse down the slope. A moment later, as Slade aimed his revolver at the girl on the ground, Slocum, his horse at a full gallop, fired into the air to distract the man.

Slade spun and for the first time saw the approaching rider. He hesitated a moment, then hauled up his weapon and fired at Slocum. The round burnt past Slocum's cheek, but he held his fire and kept coming. Slade was standing too close to the girl for Slocum to risk a shot.

Abruptly, Slade grabbed his horse's reins and vaulted into the saddle. Throwing one last wild shot over his shoulder at Slocum, he headed north. He had disappeared beyond the ridge by the time Slocum slipped from his saddle and knelt beside the unconscious woman.

She was lying face up, her magnificent crown of raven-black hair spilled upon the grassy sward under her head. Slocum was struck at once by her beauty. He took both her shoulders in his hands and shook her gently. After a moment her eyelids flickered, then opened. She stared up at him in confusion, then looked fearfully about him—for Slade, Slocum had no doubt.

"He's gone," Slocum told her. "Slade Banner just rode off. You all right?"

She sat up and nodded. Wincing, her hand flew up to grab the top of her head. "It feels like he cracked my head open."

"Lay back down," he said.

Carefully, she did as he told her. Slocum felt her head and came to the bump on her skull. It was a large one, and getting larger. Slade could have fractured her skull, but Slocum did not think so. Her thick carpet of dark hair had probably saved her.

"You should lie still," he told her. "That was a nasty crack you took."

"Who are you?"

"Name's Slocum, ma'am. John Slocum. And who might you be?"

"I am Maria Coleman. I own the Lazy C."

"That feller beatin' on you—I know him well enough. He's Slade Banner. He work for you or something?"

"He was my foreman," she said bitterly.

"Was, you say?"

"I just fired him!" she snapped.

Slocum nodded. That explained the man's rage.

Glancing past her at the ranch buildings in the valley below, he realized he would have to get a wagon or a buggy from one of the barns.

Standing up, he said, "I'm going to ride down there and bring back a buggy."

"But I can ride," she protested.

He smiled. "Yes, I suppose you could, but you might do your head considerable damage if you did. Slade scrambled your brains some. You don't want to shake them up any more for a while."

"Are you a doctor?"

"No, Miss Coleman, but I know this kind of injury. I've had it myself. I'm only telling you what one doc told me. He was a smart one. Came all the way from the East, and he didn't get his sheepskin in the mail."

"All right," she said. "Go get the wagon."

He lifted from his belt the .44 he had taken from the sheriff and handed it to her. "In case that son of a bitch comes back," he told her.

She smiled wanly as she took it. "Thanks."

He mounted up and rode the half mile to the Lazy C. The big main house was palatial, the barns huge, and all the fences and corrals well kept. It was an impressive, prosperous-looking ranch, he noted as he rode through the gate leading into the main compound.

Three hands appeared with rifles in their hands and started across the yard to intercept him as he headed for the main house. Another ranch hand, an old, stove-up cowboy—obviously the wrangler—was in the act of leading a fine bay into one of the barns when Slocum rode into the compound. As the wrangler left the bay and started toward Slocum, the smithy left the blacksmith shed, a large hammer in his hand. A black man at least six feet tall, he was bare from the waist up, his heavily muscled torso gleaming with sweat.

Slocum pulled up and waited for the three men to reach him. When they did, he dismounted. "No need to bother with them weapons," he told them.

"Who're you?" one of them asked.

"What's important right now is the owner of the Lazy C, Miss Coleman. She's been hurt."

"What's that you say?" asked the wrangler as he hurried up.

"Miss Coleman's been hurt," Slocum told the old man. "I need a wagon or a buggy to carry her. Go hitch one up. I don't think she should ride."

"Where is she?" asked the blacksmith. Like the others, he was making no effort at all to hide his suspicion. The other three men, Slocum noticed, had still not lowered their rifles.

"Back there on the slope," Slocum told the blacksmith. "And I'd like your help lifting her into the wagon."

"She fall off her horse or something?"

"She was clubbed down."

"What's that?" he asked incredulously.

"You heard me," Slocum said shortly.

"Who did it?"

"Slade Banner."

"You must be crazy!" one of the men with a rifle said. To Slocum, his pale, unshaven face seemed vaguely familiar. He had limped slightly on his way across the compound.

"Why is that so hard to believe?"

"Because Slade Banner's the Lazy C ramrod, mister. That's why!"

"Not now, he isn't," snapped Slocum. "Miss Coleman fired him. I figure that's why he struck her down."

The five men seemed confused. They looked unhappily at each other. The foundation under their snug little world had suddenly shifted alarmingly.

Slocum was losing patience. There was no telling how badly the girl had been hurt. He had left her alone up there with only the sheriff's .44 to protect her in case Slade Banner came back.

"Damn it!" he said. "Don't you men care about Maria Coleman? I told you, she's been hurt!" Slocum turned on the wrangler, who had as yet made no move at all to go back to the barn for a wagon. "What the hell are you waiting for?" Slocum demanded. "Didn't you hear me? Hitch up a wagon. That woman is all alone up there."

Still the old man, looking unhappily around him at the others, hesitated.

"You heard him, Andy," said the black. "Go hitch up that flatbed."

That seemed to be enough for the wrangler. He turned and hurried back across the compound toward the barn.

The blacksmith turned to Slocum. "You said you wanted me to go with you?"

Slocum nodded. "And I would like your friends

here to put down their weapons. It ain't very hospitable."

"Hell! We don't know you," said the fellow with the unshaven face. "You come in here tellin' us Slade is fired and Miss Maria hurt. How do we know this ain't some kind of trick?"

"What kind of trick would it be?"

The man frowned. "Damn it! How would I know?"

The black said to him, "Put down the rifle, Will. We got to see about Miss Maria first off." Then he glanced back at Slocum. "You got a name, mister?"

"Slocum. What's yours?"

"Ben Franklin."

Slocum did not smile. The three men slowly, warily lowered their rifles.

The wrangler led a horse out of the barn and proceeded to hitch it to a flatbed standing nearby. Slocum led his pony over to the wrangler when the fellow was finished and told him to grain and water it. Then he stepped up onto the wagon seat and grabbed the reins. Ben climbed up beside him. Slapping the reins, Slocum drove the wagon out of the compound.

They found Maria lying, unconscious again, where Slocum had left her, the .44 Slocum had given her gleaming in the grass beside her. With great gentleness, Ben picked Maria up and put her carefully down on the bed of the wagon. Slocum suggested he remain there beside her. Ben nodded without looking away from the unconscious woman.

Doing his best to avoid any sudden bumps or deep depressions, Slocum drove the wagon back to the ranch. Once there, he pulled up in front of the big house. An impassive Indian woman as big around and as shapeless as a water barrel was standing on the veranda. Slocum recognized her Shoshone blood at once and noted the alarm in her black eyes.

Lifting Maria carefully from the wagon, Ben carried her up the steps. The housekeeper moved ahead of him, opened the door, and led the way up to Maria's bedroom. Slocum followed them up the stairs.

Maria was still unconscious when Ben put her down. The Shoshone woman studied her mistress for a moment, then hurried from the room. What she intended to do, Slocum had no idea. He thanked Ben with a nod. The black man backed out of the room and closed the door behind him. Slocum slumped into a cushioned rocker by the bed, his eyes on the injured woman. Her lovely face was unnaturally pale.

The Indian housekeeper returned with a pan of water and fresh towels folded over her arm. Without a glance at Slocum, she set the pan down upon a nightstand beside the bed, dipped the towels into the water, and began placing cold compresses on Maria's brow. Satisfied that all that could be done was being done, Slocum got up and left.

Downstairs the four Lazy C hands were waiting for him in front of the veranda. The unshaven fellow with the slight limp—the one Ben had addressed earlier as Will—spoke up first. He was still holding his rifle. "You got any proof of what you said about Slade Banner?"

"Proof enough. He and his sidekick tried to kill me not long ago. I came along at an awkward time, while they were getting ready to rustle a herd of cattle. They thought I was the law."

This laconic statement astonished Ben, the wrangler, and the two other men.

It did not, however, appear to surprise Will. His expression just grew a bit more surly. "You expect us to believe that, do you?" he asked.

"I don't care whether you believe it or not. But I suspect that your foreman's rustling is what caused Maria to fire him. If I hadn't come along when I did, he would have killed her."

"This is pretty hard to believe, mister," said the wrangler unhappily. He ran a long, shaky hand through his thatch of white hair. He seemed ready to cry.

"Well, *I* believe it," said Ben.

"You believe this stranger?" the unshaven fellow demanded.

"Sure."

"Why?"

Ben spat a black spear of tobacco juice at a spot a few inches in front of the wrangler's feet. "Because I know Slade Banner, that's why." Ben glanced at the other two. One was obviously the cook, the other his young helper. This last ranch hand could not have been more than seventeen. "And you fellows know what a grand fellow Slade is, too," he told them.

Sheepishly, the two men nodded.

But Will was not so easily convinced. "He's been my ramrod for close on to four years," Will sputtered indignantly. "You can't just take this stranger's word."

"His name is John Slocum," said Ben. "He ain't

a stranger no more. If he didn't tell us about Miss Maria, she'd still be up there, lyin' unconscious on the ground with no one to help her."

"Maybe he's the one did it. How do we know it was Slade? I tell you, it's just his word!" Will persisted.

Ben looked coolly at Will. "Well, his word is good enough for me."

"Bullshit!" exploded Will.

"So what do you suggest?"

"I say we keep this fellow locked up while I go find Slade and get to the bottom of this," Will said.

As he spoke, he brought up his rifle once again and aimed it at Slocum's gut. With startling speed, Ben reached out and slapped down the rifle barrel. Twisting it almost casually from Will's grasp, he tossed the rifle to Slocum.

"Go find Slade, Will," Slocum told him. "When you do, tell him John Slocum is waiting for him at the Lazy C."

Will was still carrying a sidearm. For a moment it appeared he would go for it. Then he licked his lips and stepped back. With a bitter nod to Ben and then to Slocum, he started for the barn.

"I'll be back," he promised, "with Slade. Then we'll settle up with both of you."

As he rode out a moment later, Slocum turned to Ben. "He seemed vaguely familiar. Who is he? What's his name?"

"Will. Will Bright," the blacksmith replied.

"Jimmy Bright his brother?"

"Yes."

"I see," Slocum said, watching Will ride out. "I guess he will be back, at that." He turned to Ben. "You got a sidearm?"

"A Colt .44."

"Know how to use it?"

"Just try me, Slocum."

"I want you to ride with me, then."

"Where we goin'?"

"That depends on Will. But I figure there's a pretty good chance he might take us to Slade Banner."

"I'll saddle up," Ben said, and hurried off.

Slocum turned to the wrangler. "That pony of mine's earned himself a rest. Find me a good horse and saddle him."

As the wrangler hurried across the compound toward the barn, Slocum turned his attention to the two remaining ranch hands. They licked their lips nervously as he regarded them.

"Get all the firepower you can," he told them, "and wait here on this porch until Ben and I get back. If Slade returns before we do, hold him off as long you can. Remember, he already tried to kill Maria Coleman once. Don't let him get another chance."

The cook cleared his throat. "We won't let the son of a bitch near her," he promised.

His youthful helper nodded in solemn agreement.

"Fine," Slocum said.

It was obvious that the two were frightened half out of their wits, but Slocum figured their anxiety would serve to keep them alert. Slocum considered it highly unlikely that Slade would manage to slip past himself and Ben. But if Slade did decide to ride back to the Lazy C to finish what he had started, Slocum was reasonably certain these two were loyal enough not to give Maria up without a fight.

That was the best he could hope for in such an eventuality.

7

When Slade got back to his men, Sheriff Busher was waiting for him. The big man was astride his horse in front of one of the camp fires. Ignoring the anxious Carvalho, who was riding over to intercept him, Slade rode across the flat and reined up alongside the sheriff. Slade could see trouble in the way Busher sat slumped in his saddle, and he was pretty sure he knew what the trouble was.

"What is it, Busher?" Slade asked. "What brings you up here?"

"I got some bad news, Slade."

"Spill it."

"Jimmy's dead."

"Damn it! How'd it happen?"

"Jimmy tried to take Slocum while he was sleeping upstairs in Mandy's place over the restaurant. But the son of a bitch must have been waiting for him. They exchanged shots. It sounded like a Mexican revolution in there for a while. When I got up there, Jimmy had a hole in his chest and Slocum was standing over him with a smoking gun in his hand."

"Wait'll Will hears this."

The lawman nodded gloomily. "That son of a bitch Slocum worked me over some, too. He broke loose while I was taking him down to the lockup. Knocked me clear down the back steps. I must've cracked a couple of ribs. I can hardly ride." He looked plaintively at Slade, angling for some appreciation for his riding out to warn Slade despite his pitiable condition.

But Slade was not concerned with the sheriff's condition. His mind was busy taking stock of the situation. He had expected what Busher had just told him. The moment Slade had seen Slocum bearing down on him back at the Lazy C, he had realized that Jimmy must have come a cropper. What concerned Slade now was how to deal with Slocum. If this fellow Slocum was not a federal marshal, he sure as hell was no ordinary drifter.

"What do you want me to do, Slade?" Busher asked bleakly.

"Go on back to Coleman Flats and bury Jimmy. And tell Jenny not to expect me tonight. I got urgent business, tell her."

"Sure, Slade."

Painfully, the big man pulled his mount around and rode carefully from the encampment. He must be hurting bad, Slade noted. The outsized lawman rode as if he were made of eggshells.

Antonio Carvalho rode up, his long, mournful

face filled with concern. "Did you find Maria?" he asked. "Was she the rider Mel saw on the ridge?"

At least for now, Slade needed Carvalho's support. Better than a third of the Lazy C riders were loyal to the old man personally. Accordingly, Slade had prepared a lie brazen enough, he hoped, to gain him the time he needed.

"It was her, all right," he told Antonio. "But before I could catch up to her, this fellow Slocum intercepted her. He now has Maria hostage."

"Hostage?"

"Yes."

"Mother of God, what does he want?"

"He wants these cattle, damn it! He's a hired gun working for the drovers we took this herd from. Unless we free Maria and kill him, he'll bring the rest of those drovers down on us."

"You're sure he has Maria hostage?"

"I saw him up ahead of me, talking to her. Whatever he told her, there was a struggle. He slugged her, hauled her over his saddle, and rode on ahead of me to the ranch. I tried to overtake him, but I was too far behind. When I reached the compound, he was holed up in the main house. Ben, Will, and the others were standing around wondering what to do."

"I do not understand. What would he want with Maria?"

"She must have told him she was the owner of the Lazy C. When he saw me coming after him, he must've figured the only chance he had was to use Maria as a hostage to gain time."

"We must do nothing that would endanger Maria," Carvalho warned.

"I know that."

"So what do you propose?"

"Get the men together and ride back. Now. Surround the compound and make Slocum show himself. As soon as he does, we'll cut him down."

Carvalho frowned. "Ugly," he said.

"You got a better idea?"

"Let me ride back, reason with him."

"You ready to give him back this herd?" Slade asked.

"Are you so sure that is what he wants? Perhaps a payment of some kind."

"There's no bribing this son of a bitch. And don't forget, he's already killed Jimmy."

"It's Maria I am concerned about, Slade."

The old man had suddenly developed a backbone, Slade noted. It was the perceived threat to Maria that had done it.

"Don't you think that's what I'm thinking about, too?" he asked. "Hell, Antonio, you know how I feel about Maria."

The old man's eyes grew cold. "It is that woman in Coleman Flats you care about. Jenny Warren."

"She's just someone to keep me warm for now."

Carvalho drew himself up to his full height. "This conversation is stupid. And we waste time. We will do as you say. Return to the ranch and surround it. This madman cannot hole up forever with Maria. Let us go now."

Slade nodded. "I'll round up the men on this side

of the canyon, and you get the ones in the hills over there. When you see Mel, tell him I want to see him."

Carvalho nodded and rode off across the shallow stream. Slade watched him go. The old Mexican was all of a sudden a problem. Slade's hope was that he could manage to keep the stupid bastard from catching on before he dealt with Slocum. Otherwise, Slade would just have to cut the old man down.

He had gathered about ten of his riders when he saw Will Bright cutting through the canyon toward him. Leaving his riders, Slade pulled his horse around and splashed across the shallow stream to intercept Will.

Pulling up excitedly, Will said, "We got trouble, Slade! Maria's been hurt—hurt bad. And the fellow who brought her in says *you* did it. He says you clubbed her."

Slade smiled thinly. "Keep your voice down, Will. I know all about that son of a bitch. Is his name Slocum?"

"That's him. John Slocum."

"All right, now sit steady and listen to me, Will. I got some bad news for you. That son of a bitch Slocum has already killed your brother."

Will's face went gray and for a moment Slade thought he was going to fall from his saddle. Slumping forward, Will stared bleakly at the foreman. "I knew he was trouble," Will rasped miserably. "Jesus, Slade—when did this happen?"

"Last night I sent Jimmy into Coleman Flats to take Slocum. Jimmy wanted to do it. He considered it unfinished business. The sheriff was the one who told me. He just left. He said Slocum shot Jimmy. If you want, you can ride on into Coleman Flats and see to Jimmy's burial."

Will nodded numbly. "Maybe I'll do that," he said. "But what are you going to do about Slocum?"

"Get the men together and ride back to the ranch."

"What then?"

Slade smiled coldly. "We'll surround the place. I told Carvalho that Slocum is holding Maria hostage."

Will frowned. "Carvalho might go for that. When I left the ranch, Maria was upstairs in her bedroom, unconscious. If she's still out when you get there, it'll be your word against his."

"Fine. But we won't spend any time trading charges."

"What do you mean?"

"The minute Slocum shows, we'll cut him down."

Will looked craftily at Slade. "Was it you hit Maria, like Slocum said?"

"It was. She was prepared to fire me, expose every damn one of us. She gave me no choice. I would have killed her if Slocum hadn't come along when he did."

Will took a deep breath. "I think maybe I'll ride with you then," he said, his eyes gleaming meanly. "I want to be there when Slocum gets it."

It was not difficult for Slade Banner to understand how Will felt. "Join the other riders," he told Will. "Be careful what you say. Make sure it backs up what I've already told them—that Slocum's taken Maria hostage and is holed up in the ranch house."

Will nodded and rode on past Slade across the stream to join the rest of the Lazy C riders who were coming down from the hills with Carvalho. Watching him go, Slade felt a small elation building inside him.

What Will had just told him had given him an idea. As soon as they reached the ranch and cut down Slocum, Banner would enter the ranch house and finish Maria with another blow to the head. The dead Slocum could be blamed for her death. And, if the few hands at the Lazy C protested, it would be Slade's word against that of a dead man. Then Slade would only have to worry about Carvalho. But not for long. Slade did not think he would have much difficulty convincing the old, dispirited Mexican to sell out at a reasonable price.

This new plan warmed the cockles of Banner's heart. He found himself wondering how Jenny would like being the wife of a big rancher. She was always telling him how much she hated running the saloon.

Slocum and Ben, astride their mounts, looked down from the same ridge Maria had used earlier that morning. Ben was dressed in a sheepskin jacket similar to Slocum's, riding boots, and a flat-crowned black Stetson. His blacksmith's shoulders stretched the jacket to its limit. On his right hip, resting in a polished black leather cut-down army holster, sat a gleaming pearl-handled Colt.

They had followed Will Bright to this wilderness of hills and canyons and had watched from the ridge while Will rode up and conferred with Slade Banner.

It was not lost on either of them that as soon as Will spoke to Banner, the ranch foreman proceeded to gather his riders. They were just about ready to move out.

"Who's that tall rider alongside Slade?" Slocum asked Ben. "The one with the sombrero."

"Antonio Carvalho. Maria's father brought him up from Texas with him. He is devoted to Maria. I sure don't understand how he could be in on this rustling with Slade." Ben shook his head gloomily.

"At the moment, he probably knows nothing about Maria."

"I don't see how he could. Slade sure as hell wouldn't have told him. Not the truth of it, anyway."

"You think it might make a difference when he finds out?"

"Slocum, I never saw a man take better care of a girl than Carvalho has done with Maria. After that big Texan died he was like a father to her. And he never forgot he was her servant."

With Slade and the Mexican at the head of the column, the Lazy C hands were riding into a steep-sided canyon below them. They were heading south, back toward the Lazy C.

"Ben, it looks to me like Slade's fixing to move against the ranch now. He's got the men and the firepower. If he succeeds, I wouldn't give much for Maria's life—or for Carvalho's, either, if what you say is true."

"Hell, Slocum, Slade wouldn't dare. Not all those men down there are loyal to Slade. At least half of them would follow that old Mexican straight into hell."

"They might have to," Slocum commented. "Let's go."

As he followed Slocum off the ridge, the blacksmith asked, "What've you got in mind?"

"I'll explain on the way. Come on."

Slocum saw Slade glance up and go for his sidearm. He fired. The round missed Slade, but sliced neatly through his reins. In the narrow, twisting canyon, the rifle's detonation was enough to spook his mount. The animal reared, and without his reins Slade tumbled ignominiously back off his horse.

Riding beside Slade, Carvalho went for his own sidearm, but Ben's voice cut through the echo of the rifle shot.

"Don't reach for your gun, Señor Carvalho!" he cried.

"And stay on the ground, Slade!" Slocum snapped.

Looking up, Slade saw Slocum standing on a ledge in full sight, his rifle still tucked into his shoulder. The muzzle was aimed at Slade's head, and the sight of it caused Slade to go suddenly gray.

Behind him in the narrow passageway, the Lazy C riders were shouting excitedly to each other as a few tried to push through to join Slade.

"Tell the rest of your men to hold up!" Slocum shouted.

Slade yelled at his men to keep back. The shouting ceased and the sound of their scrambling horses came to a halt as well.

"I should have killed you, Slade," Slocum said. "But I find it hard to kill a man in cold blood. Maybe the next time I won't feel that way."

"Damn you! What do you want?"

"I want you to tell Señor Carvalho what you did to Maria. And tell it loud enough so some of those Lazy C hands behind you can hear it too."

Despite his terror, Slade was in no mood to confess the truth. "I didn't do nothin' to Maria!" he cried. "It was you! You took her hostage!"

Slocum fired a second time. The round ripped through the sleeve of Slade's right arm, creasing his muscle. It could only have been a flesh wound, but Slade grabbed at his arm, yelping in pain. Slocum saw Slade's knees start to buckle.

"Tell the truth!" Slocum warned.

"I had no choice!" Slade wailed. "She was going to fire me—all of us. And she was going to tell everyone in the valley how we've been stocking her range. She was going to ruin us. She had no appreciation of what Antonio and I have done for the Lazy C!"

"So you clubbed her, struck her down, and would have killed her if I hadn't stopped you," Slocum said.

"No! I wouldn't have killed her—I swear!"

Carvalho turned his horse so he could look down at Slade. His face was pale with fury. "It was you who struck Maria down. You lied to me!"

"Damn it, Carvalho," Slade told him, "you heard

what I said. She would have blamed you, too. You would have been left with nothing after all these years."

"Insect!" Carvalho cried, grabbing for his gun. Belatedly, Slade did the same. But Ben's sharp voice stopped them both.

"Freeze! Both of you!"

Though Ben was hidden so well in the rocks that neither man could see him, it was obvious he was close enough to hit what he aimed at. Carvalho and Slade did as they were told.

"Slade!" Slocum barked. "Hand your gun to Carvalho!"

Slade handed his gun to the old Mexican, all the while looking frantically above him at the sheer walls of the canyon, desperate to locate Ben's hiding place. Meanwhile, four Lazy C riders had crowded up past the rocks behind them and were now peering warily up at Slocum.

"Carvalho!" Slocum said. "March Slade up here to me."

Carvalho dismounted and began to shove Slade roughly up the steep slope. As he did so, the canyon floor below them slowly filled with Lazy C riders, all of them with their faces upturned. Many of them had heard what Slade had said, and they were talking excitedly among themselves. Others were arguing bitterly. Slocum, Carvalho, and Slade were the only figures visible to them. Ben still remained hidden from sight.

Slade and Carvalho had almost reached the ledge

when Will Bright nudged his horse out in front of
the other riders, drew his gun, and fired up at Slocum.

But it was old Carvalho who sagged. Slocum
returned Will's fire, but Will flung his horse about
and was out of sight behind a wall of rock before
Slocum could get off another shot. In the confusion,
Slade scrambled back down the trail, jumped onto
Carvalho's horse, and charged back through the milling
riders. More than a few of them tried to stop
Slade, but he beat them off and followed Will.
About a dozen riders—after momentary confusion—
wheeled their horses about and galloped off after
their fleeing ramrod.

Slocum, Ben, the wounded Carvalho, and the seven
riders loyal to Carvalho arrived back at the Lazy C
later that same day. As they rode into the compound,
they were all relieved to see Maria Coleman and the
Shoshone housekeeper sitting in wicker chairs on the
veranda. A towel had been wrapped about Maria's
head. Obviously still weak, she did not get up to
greet them as they rode toward her across the
compound.

Pulling up in front of the veranda, Ben and Slocum
helped Carvalho down off his horse. The housekeeper
led them into the house, a concerned Maria
following. Carvalho was brought into his bedroom
behind the kitchen. As Slocum had already ascertained,
the round had gone through his left side. It was a
reasonably clean wound, and Carvalho had remained
conscious during the ride back, but he had lost con-

siderable blood and was quite weak by the time they put him down.

Once again the Shoshone woman went to work, this time with towels and steaming hot water. Satisfied that Carvalho was being cared for, Ben and the other riders dispersed to take care of their horses. Slocum suggested to Maria that she return to the porch with him. He had much to tell her.

When he finished relating how he and Ben had forced Slade into admitting what he had done to her in front of Carvalho and the Lazy C riders, she was quite a sober young lady. "So Antonio is still loyal to me, of course," he said. "But he was part of this rustling. He knew all along, and he did nothing to warn me."

"I imagine Slade sucked him in gradually, asking him to look the other way whenever Slade brought in a few mavericks, and before he knew it, he was part of Slade's operation. He had no wish to hurt you, I'm sure."

She shook her head in sorrow. "He has been like a father to me."

"Then don't go too hard with him. I'm sure he is punishing himself far more than you could."

She nodded, sighing, then looked at him sharply. "What do we do now? I told you what Slade threatened. And he won't stop at burning me out or killing my horses. He's got at least a dozen men still loyal to him—and that's not counting the sheriff and his men."

"I suggest we look for allies," Slocum said.

"You mean the other ranchers in this valley?"

"Yes. If you'll give me a map of some kind, I'll visit each ranch personally."

"But they hate the Lazy C. And now that I know why, I don't blame them."

"It's a different poker deck we're dealing now, Maria. Slade is not your foreman, and the Lazy C is no longer a market for rustled cattle. The other cattlemen in the valley won't see the Lazy C as such an unfair threat to them any more."

"When will you leave?"

"First thing in the morning. Slade will be making his move before long, I figure, so we have to move fast."

"Who will you leave in charge while you're gone?" she asked.

Without bothering to consult him in the matter, Slocum realized, Maria had made him the Lazy C's new ramrod. For a moment he considered protesting; then he shrugged inwardly and decided to save any protests for later. With old Carvalho out of action, Maria sure as hell did need a ramrod. It wouldn't hurt for him to take the job for a while, at least until he got his hands on Slade again.

"I'll be leaving Ben in charge," he told her.

"But he's the blacksmith!"

Slocum shrugged. "I think he'll make a fine ramrod, at least for now. He handled himself well enough this afternoon."

She considered that for a moment, then shrugged. "If you say so."

He smiled. "How's your head?"

"I've still got a headache, but it's not so intense. And I'm not dizzy any more," she replied.

"Just the same, try to get as much rest as you can."

"Don't worry."

He got up.

"Where are you going?" Maria asked him.

"I want to see to my horse."

"The wrangler will tend to that. Sit back down. I want to know more about you—and where you came from."

"That might take some time."

"I don't care."

"Is that an order?"

Impishly, her eyes alight, she nodded. "Yes," she said, "it is."

Slocum sat back down and began to talk. It was dusk when the cook rang the triangle outside the bunkhouse and reminded the two of them how hungry they were. Still talking quietly, Slocum and Maria went into the house to find that the Indian housekeeper, Little Raven, had set the table and was about ready to call them in to eat.

Before they sat down, Maria asked Raven about Carvalho.

"He sleeps now," the woman replied. "And he no longer bleeds. Eat."

Relieved, Slocum sat down to a hearty meal. All the time he was aware that to look too deeply into Maria's dark eyes was a dizzying experience. In fact, despite his attempt to cool himself down a bit, the blood in his veins was racing feverishly. And

Maria's glances were doing nothing to help him cool off.

She was an exquisitely lovely young lady, and he had no wish to disappoint her, nor did he want to deprive himself. But there were, he had discovered, two nagging hurdles to be cleared. The first was that Maria Coleman was still too weak from her injuries for any passionate exertions. The second was that she was still a virgin.

Maria had not been at all shy about making that point.

8

Slade Banner was trying to think, but he was having trouble doing so. Sitting at the same table were Will Bright and the sheriff. The two men were arguing bitterly, and had been for the past half hour. Will had consumed enough whiskey to make him dangerous, but the sheriff seemed unaware of his danger as he insisted that Will was crazy to blame him for his brother's death.

"You was here, you big, fat son of a bitch," Will snarled meanly. "You should've gone up there with Jimmy—backed his play."

"He would have none of it," the sheriff protested. "He told me to mind my own business."

"Business!" Will cried, slapping his empty whiskey glass down on the table so hard it sounded like a gunshot. "None of your business! Damn it, you was the one should've taken care of Slocum, not my brother!"

Slade decided it was time to end this. "Shut up,

Will. You've said enough—and maybe you've drunk enough, too. I sent Jimmy in here to take care of Slocum. You want to blame someone, blame me."

Will turned his head to glare unhappily at Slade. He reminded Slade of a bull pawing the ground, getting ready to make his charge.

"Get out of here and get some sleep," Slade told him.

Will swallowed. "Where the hell am I goin' to find a place this late?"

"Find a woman and sleep with her."

Will looked unhappily around him. The Horse Head was crowded with those Lazy C riders who had stayed with Slade. Most of them had a girl at their elbow, some more than one. This sudden, unexpected holiday from the routine of the Lazy C was bothering Slade's men not at all. But each time Will caught the eye of a girl, she looked quickly away and clung a little close to the man she was with. For most of the evening, Will had revealed only a ferocious, whiskey-fueled belligerence, and no girl in the place wanted anything to do with him.

Will looked back at Slade. "I saved your ass this afternoon, Slade. Slocum had you by the short hair. I was the one got you free."

"That's right. And you also shot Antonio Carvalho. Nice going."

"Shit! That old Mex! What do you care about him?"

"Maria cares about him. If Antonio dies, any chance I might have had of reasoning with that girl, of maybe buying her out peaceful, will be gone. And I have you to thank for that."

"Your chances were already gone, damn it!"

Slade sighed wearily. "Just get out of here, Will. Do what I said. Go find yourself a woman. I'm tired of you. Everyone in this place is tired of you."

Slade spoke in a cold, unemotional tone, but his eyes had the lidded, sleepy look of a snake just before it strikes. Will caught the look and got to his feet. Swaying slightly, he turned and limped from the saloon. As the batwings slapped shut behind him, an almost audible sigh of relief swept the saloon.

Jenny had kept her distance since Slade entered with the sheriff and Will Bright, content to remain behind the bar. Now she came over to Slade's table and sat down.

"I wanted to stop serving him," she told Slade, "but I didn't know but what he might have started shooting up the place."

Slade nodded. "Jimmy I could handle. Will is a wild one. He's been steaming ever since he broke his hip trying to ride Maria's stallion. And now this."

The sheriff, sensing that Slade wanted to speak privately with Jenny Warren, excused himself and left the saloon.

Watching the sheriff leave, Slade muttered, "I hope to hell Will doesn't decide to continue the argument with Busher out there."

"Hell, in Will's condition," Jenny said, "he won't pose much of a threat to Busher."

"I'm not so sure of that."

Jenny reached out and placed her hand on Slade's forearm. "I know you got trouble all of a sudden, Slade. But, after all this time, I'm glad to see you."

Slade smiled crookedly at Jenny. "Every cloud has a silver lining, eh?" He patted her hand, then leaned back in his chair, an intent frown on his face. "Trouble is, I got to move fast if I don't want to lose everything I been building these past five years." He shook his head and blew out his cheeks. Then he glanced at the woman. "You met Slocum, didn't you?"

"Yes, I did. I joined him over at that table in the back."

"What do you think of him?"

"I think you got a wildcat by the tail. Or maybe a panther, by the look of him. He's big enough and mad enough to rassle a grizzly and win. I didn't like the gleam in those mean green eyes of his. I got the feeling he just doesn't know how to quit."

"That's him, all right," Slade muttered. "Hell, by all rights he should be dead. Jimmy saw his horse go down with that herd thunderin' at his back. Jimmy had no reason to lie about that. And now the son of a bitch shows up here." He shook his head at the thought. "You're right. I got me a panther by the tail."

"So what are you going to do?"

"That's what I been tryin' to figure. Right now Slocum is probably holed up at the Lazy C with Maria and the few riders who are still loyal to her. I don't figure Carvalho will be much help. For all I know, he's dead already. Maria tried to tell me she could get help from the other ranches, The Bench and the Bar N. I doubt it. And I don't see Slim Hennessey of the Bar O offering to help her, either."

"So she's alone."

"Yes. And I guess my job is to see she remains that way, then go on in and take her—and Slocum."

"You make it sound like a war," Jenny said.

"That's what it is. A range war."

"Maybe you should just pull out, Slade."

He looked at her in some surprise. "Pull out?"

"Yes."

"After all this?"

"Slade, forget the Lazy C. I got enough—more than enough—saved up for the both of us. We could go to San Francisco."

Slade shook his head. "No woman is going to take care of me, Jenny."

She pulled back, her face twisting in exasperation. "Men!" she said. "You men and your stupid pride."

"It's what gives us backbone," Slade told her. "You wouldn't have nothin' to do with a man who didn't have it. And you know it."

Jenny had no response to that. Slade was sure she recognized the truth in what he said. But he had no desire to argue with the woman. It had been a long hard week, most of it spent in the saddle, and he was looking forward to the comfort Jenny was eager to provide for him upstairs in that big bed of hers.

But he was not ready to go upstairs yet. He needed to get things straight in his own mind first. What he wanted was a clear picture of what lay ahead for him. Until he could see what his next move had to be, relaxation was impossible for him.

Jenny cleared her throat. "Suppose the other ranchers in the valley do decide to rally around Maria?" she suggested carefully. "Slade, I know you don't think they will, but just suppose they do? Maybe this Slocum will be able to convince them."

Slade frowned at her. She had a point. He knew the other ranchers hated the Lazy C enough to stay clear of Maria. He and his men had done their best to make the ranchers feel that way. Still, things were different now. Though he was sure nothing could make those other ranchers join up with the Lazy C, not too long ago, after collecting this last herd, he had been just as certain he had the world by the tail.

"Maybe you've got a point," he replied.

"Of course, you may be right about that swine, Hennessey," Jenny went on, "but I'm not so sure about Gulick and Neuberger. I've heard them in here, Slade. It's you they blame, not Maria. Maybe this chance to join forces against you is just what they've been waiting for."

"And all it would take would be for Slocum to convince them."

"Yes."

"Then the fat *would* be in the fire. I'd sure as hell have to move fast then."

"Or make sure of Gulick and Neuberger," she replied.

"How do you propose I do that?"

She shrugged.

He looked away from her, his mind racing. He

could threaten The Bench and the Bar N. And maybe he could get Hennessey's Bar O to go along with him on that. Slim was contrary and mean enough to consider backing his play against those other two ranchers. But what could he use to threaten the others?

Then Slade had an inspiration. He grinned at Jenny.

"Now what?" she asked warily.

"I have a way to make sure of Gulick and Neuberger."

"What is it?"

"Simple. I'll close the town to them. They'll get no more supplies."

"Can you do that?"

"I own the sheriff. He's the law in this town. And Potter and Phillips will do as I say. You know that."

Jenny nodded.

Potter ran the only mill and Phillips the general store. Between the two of them, these merchants supplied whatever the ranchers needed, as well as whatever was needed by the town's saloons and restaurants. Both merchants were wanted men elsewhere—Potter for embezzlement, Phillips for a swindling scheme that had gone awry. It was Slade who had brought them here and bankrolled them. In the years that followed, Coleman Flats became a way station for every gunslick and killer west of the Mississippi, providing Slade with an ample supply of men desperate enough for his various enterprises. In fact, each Lazy C rider who had remained loyal to him earlier that same day had come to Coleman Flats to escape the law, just as Slade himself had, all those years ago.

Slade would have no trouble closing the mill and the general store to Gulick and Neuberger—and to Hennessey's Bar O, if it came to that.

"It'll work," Slade said emphatically. "I'm sure of it."

Jenny shrugged. "Maybe it will."

"Get Tim. I want him to take messages to those ranchers. And I want him to ride out now."

"You want me to write the messages for you?"

"Yes."

"I'll send for Tim," she said, getting to her feet, "and go look for a pen and some paper."

Slade watched her go, satisfied with his plan.

The note he would send Gulick and Neuberger would be different from the one for Hennessey. The two ranchers would be told that unless they kept out of his scrap with Maria and the Lazy C, he would see to it that they were unable to trade in town, that their credit would no longer be accepted at the mill or the general store. And, if that didn't do it, Slade would make Potter and Phillips call in the two ranchers' paper.

His note to Hernessey would tell him that if he joined Slade in his battle with Maria Coleman, Slade would give him a quarter of the Lazy C's stock to run on his range. Furthermore, Slade would pledge Hennessey any help he might need in his constant running battle with Gulick and Neuberger.

Slade leaned back in his chair and reached for his drink. He was beginning to feel more relaxed by the minute. As soon as he sent Tim on his way, he guessed it might be time for him to go upstairs with Jenny. He emptied the stein down his gullet, wiped off his mouth with the back of his hand, and smacked his lips.

He was ready now.

Not much later, on his way past the restaurant across from the Horse Head, Will Bright pulled up woozily and watched Tim gallop out of town, heading for the valley. Will was considerably drunker than he had been when Slade sent him away from the Horse Head. And he was even angrier.

After watching Tim disappear into the night, Will turned and almost fell to the ground. He managed to reach out and grab hold of the side of the restaurant. Glancing through the window facing the street, he saw Mandy O'Brien putting a plate down in front of a customer.

Will remembered then that Slocum had been upstairs in Mandy's bedroom when he gunned down Jimmy Bright. Mandy O'Brien had always been too good for either him or Jimmy, but she had sure as hell been nice enough to that bastard, Slocum. Thinking of Mandy sleeping with the killer of his brother caused Will to seethe. An unreasonable fury swept over him. It was all he could do to keep himself from barging into the restaurant and beating the hell out of that little blonde whore.

No. There was a better way, he realized.

He passed a hand over his face and straightened up, blinking owlishly in the light that came from the street lamp. Yes, there was a much better way to punish that little bitch, and at the same time settle his score with Slocum. Hadn't Slade told him to find a girl who would give him a bed for the night? Then, afterward, he'd have just the item to perk up his buddy, Slim Hennessey. By damn! It was perfect!

Concentrating mightily, Will lurched into the alley that ran alongside the restaurant. He stumbled more than once in the dark, but he found the back steps with little difficulty and climbed them to Mandy's apartment. The door was locked. He kicked it open without pause, saw the sofa, and collapsed down onto it.

He felt himself spinning off into an alcoholic stupor, but this did not bother him. The moment Mandy found him sleeping on her couch, she'd let out a scream that would wake him up good and proper. Then he'd quiet her down and set his plan into motion. The thought of how he would quiet her down warmed him and filled him with delicious anticipation.

As he spun off into oblivion, there was a mean smile on his face.

Slocum sat up. Maria, wearing a long, pale nightdress, floated like a cloud across the room to him. Her dark hair was combed out and as she paused at the side of his bed and leaned over him, the fragrance from her long tresses caused the muscles in his groin to tighten involuntarily.

"Are you awake, John?" Maria whispered softly.

In the darkness he saw her teeth gleam as her mouth parted in a smile.

"I'm awake. Wide awake."

"Little Raven said I should join you."

"What's she got to do with this visit?" he asked.

"She said it is time I knew a man. I agree with her. For a while I toyed with the idea of allowing Slade Banner to visit with me, but I could not bring myself to do it. Raven did not like him, either. I am glad I waited. Raven said you are twice the man Slade is. She says she likes your shoulders and your eyes. She thinks you might have some Indian blood."

"The hell with what Raven thinks. What about you?"

She sat down on the bed and leaned over him, her hair covering his head and shoulders like a dark tent. Her pale face was inches from his, her dark eyes gleaming down at him. "I think Little Raven is right," she said. "And I think you should take me. Now."

"Just ease up there a moment, will you?"

"Aren't you ready?"

"It's you I am worried about. You are a virgin, and I consider this quite a responsibility. Besides, what about your injury?"

"My head is fine now," she said. She shook her hair back over her shoulders and peered down at him imperiously. "You consider me some kind of wild horse you must break? Is that it?"

He smiled. "Not break—break in."

She went to slap him and he grabbed her wrists. She started laughing and, before Slocum was entirely aware of it, she was beside him on the bed, her lips fastened to his. His own need matched hers, and in a kind of feverish frenzy both of them threw off what few clothes they wore.

A small voice deep inside Slocum told him to go slow, no matter how ready she might appear to be, and he heeded it. He answered her kiss for kiss, then began kissing her behind her ears, then on the nape of her neck, and finally on her breasts. She began to flow under him like something molten, uttering tiny, impatient cries, but he continued to heed that small voice.

"Oh, now!" she moaned. "Now! I am ready! I tell you, I am ready."

He paid no attention as his lips found her thighs, then the soft mound of her pubis, then explored further.

She began to thrust, her hands buried in his hair, her head twisting from side to side. She was beside herself. Every nerve in her body wanted something more, but Slocum was not ready to give it to her. She grew moist, and he left her pubis and moved up to her belly, kissing it passionately, then feasted on her high, soaring breasts, his tongue flicking at each erect nipple in turn with devilish efficiency. Her fists began to beat upon his back as she heaved feverishly under him.

"Damn you!" she cried. "I've seen my stallion mount his mare! You know what I want now!"

She reached down frantically and grabbed at him, closing her fist about his erection.

"This is what I want!" she cried, attempting to scoot under him.

He pulled away playfully and kissed her neck, chuckling. Her teeth closed about his earlobe and he almost cried out.

It was what he had been waiting for. He would not hurt her now. Or, if he did, she would not mind. She was ready. And so was he. With swift efficiency, he thrust his knees between her thighs. Reaching down, he found her moist warmth, then plunged down into her, almost touching bottom first time. She cried out in sudden pain. It was more a yelp than a cry. Relentlessly, he plunged again. This time he went all the way.

"Oh, my God!" she cried, flinging her arms around his neck. "My stallion! You have severed me, I swear!"

He laughed. "It only feels that way."

"What are you doing now?" she asked, eyes wide as she stared up at his heaving body.

"Don't ask," he muttered. "I'll tell you when I finish. I can't stop now."

Before he climaxed, she began to writhe once again. Soon, she was close to coming also. But it was too late for her. He was already climaxing. Her eyes grew wide in wonderment as she felt him spill his warm seed into her.

He kissed her gently on the lips. She kissed him back, murmuring happily. He made no effort to pull out, but continued to smile down at her and kiss her on the face and neck, waiting for himself to come alive again. It was not long before her warmth and the way she was returning his kisses enabled him to regain his erection. Her eyes grew wide as she felt him grow within her, and she hugged him still tighter.

This time, as he began to thrust gently, he guided her thrusts with his big hands under her buttocks. She caught on fast. Her face began to flush as a tight smile spread over her countenance. She laughed low, seductively.

"Yes," she muttered. "Yes, I can feel it now. This time I'm the one who can't stop!"

He brought her along carefully, then found himself caught up as well. Soon, they were thrusting in unison, building nicely. This time, a second before he did, she climaxed, uttering a high, exultant cry.

He came a moment later, sagged forward, then rolled off her, laughing. "There!" he said, grinning down at her. After that bugle call, I'm sure Little Raven knows that all went well. Just tell me one thing."

She clung to him, her head nestled against his chest. "Anything."

"Why do you call her Little Raven? There's nothing little about her."

"When she first came to work for us, she was no bigger than a minute. Just call her Raven, like I do. She prefers it. Now let's do that again."

"You like it, huh?"

"Of course."

"And you want to get it right, huh?"

"Yes, hurry!" Her hand went down to his crotch. "Oh, my, it's not big any more."

"Maria," Slocum said softly, "I think it is time

for me to tell you about the birds and the bees. And about men and woman, too."

"Will that make you big again?" she asked, laughing softly.

"That depends," he sighed.

"On what?"

"On how well you listen."

She snuggled still closer, and Slocum began to tell her of the first woman he had had as a young boy, in a hayloft on a hot summer afternoon. This first young lady's needs had been comparatively uncomplicated, so that it was left to the other women he discovered soon thereafter to build his expertise.

Though at first her eagerness to learn kept her alert, Maria was soon fast asleep in his arms. Before long he fell asleep himself, without having to reveal to Maria that he was only a man, not a superman.

9

One of the many streams that coiled through the valley hooked away from Slocum's trail and lost itself in the gently rolling meadowland. He stayed on the rutted trail and soon topped a rise that gave him a clear view of Sam Neuberger's Bar N. The ranch buildings sat among a stand of cottonwoods, a heavily timbered slope at its back, the mountains's flank continuing out into the valley like a giant wedge. As he rode closer, he saw that the ranch house was constructed solidly of logs and the four outbuildings of rough, unplaned lumber. The blacksmith shed was an open, three-sided affair with a tin roof. A well-kept network of pole corrals behind the two barns opened onto the horse pasture.

As he rode toward the ranch, he noted that the grass was so tall it brushed his stirrups. He caught sight of three ranch hands standing before the hitch rails in front of the house. They were watching him approach. One of them was shading his eyes with his hand. Soon a man and a woman left the house to join the three hands. From Maria's description, Slocum knew they were Neuberger and his wife, Samantha. In Neuberger's hand was what appeared to be a shotgun.

Slocum had not expected a warm welcome. As Maria had pointed out to him that morning, Bar N had had a running feud with her ranch for years now. It had something to do with a few streams bordering their land and some timber rights. Maria apologized for not knowing anything more specific than that.

Despite the shotgun, Slocum did not slacken his pace any as he rode into the compound. Pulling up before the five people, he saw fear and a grim determination stamped on Neuberger's lean, handsome face. Slocum glanced swiftly about him and saw another ranch hand peering at him from around the corner of a tool shed. This one, too, was armed.

Though it was not good manners to talk to someone on foot while still in the saddle, Slocum had the distinct impression that he was not welcome at all.

"Howdy, ma'am," he said to the woman, touching his hat brim to her. Then he smiled at Neuberger. "My name's Slocum. I come a long way to see you. Mind if I light and set a spell?"

"You from the Lazy C?" Neuberger asked.

Slocum nodded.

"Then you can light and set if you want, but I'll tell you right here and now, we're not going to take sides in any dispute you have with Slade Banner."

Slocum was astonished. Dismounting carefully,

he looked at Neuberger. "News sure travels fast in this valley."

"Yes, it does," Samantha Neuberger snapped. "Bad news especially."

She turned and led the two men into the ranch house. As Slocum entered, he was immediately impressed. Nothing was new, and little he saw was store-bought, but everything was well cared for and clean. There was not a speck of dust, and the dishes sitting face up in the crude open cupboard positively gleamed.

Neuberger sat down at the deal table and Slocum sat across from him. Fresh coffee was being kept warm on the big black wood stove against the wall. Samantha poured coffee for both men, placed a small pot of honey before them, and sat down with no cup in front of her.

"How did you learn of the Lazy C's trouble with Slade Banner?" Slocum asked.

"We heard," Neuberger said. "That's all you need to know."

Slocum smiled. "You sure don't act very friendly."

"The Lazy C has not been a very neighborly outfit, Slocum. It does my heart good to see it begin now to stew in its own juice."

"Yes," said Samantha, her dark eyes gleaming. She was a bony woman, almost as tall as her husband. Her brown hair had been gathered onto a tight bun at the back of her head. Her faded dress was immaculate and shapeless, and Slocum could not help noticing her hands. They were almost raw from the harsh soap she used. "Perhaps Maria will get down off her high horse now," she went on. "She's been lording it over this valley long enough."

"Are you sure it was her? Perhaps it was Slade, her foreman."

"It doesn't matter," snapped Neuberger. "Maria or Slade Banner or that Mexican, Carvalho. It's all the same to me."

"Perhaps if you understood what has been going on for the past four years, you might think differently."

"Slocum, it's *because* of what has been going on all that time that we feel the way we do," the rancher replied.

"Then you know about the rustling?" Slocum asked.

"Of course. There was no way that could be kept a secret."

"And you think Maria knew about it."

"If she didn't," Samantha put in, "she should have. It was *her* ranch. Slade Banner was *her* foreman."

"Well, I'm here to tell you she didn't know," Slocum said.

"It no longer matters what she knew or didn't know," Neuberger said wearily. "I told you. We are not going to get involved in this conflict between Slade and Maria."

He finished his coffee and looked coldly at Slocum, obviously expecting Slocum to drain his own cup and leave.

But Slocum did not want to give up so easily. He cleared his throat. "As soon as Maria realized how Slade had been stocking the Lazy C, she fired him," he told them. "As a result, Slade almost killed her, and one of his men has shot and seriously wounded Antonio Carvalho. If you turn your back on the Lazy C now, you will be siding with Slade Banner. As far as I am concerned, that will put you in his corner. Is that what you want?"

Both Neuberger and his wife had chosen not to respond to Slocum's remark, but Slocum thought he saw Samantha blush. Neuberger shifted unhappily and seemed about to make a rejoinder, but held himself back. He was too polite and hospitality was too much ingrained in the man for him to tell Slocum to get out. But it was obvious to Slocum that he wanted him to leave as soon as possible.

Neuberger got to his feet. "I'm afraid you caught us in the middle of a busy afternoon, Slocum. There's quite a bit of work yet to be done before sundown. I'm sure you understand."

Slocum got to his feet, finished his coffee, then strode from the kitchen. As he mounted up he looked down at Neuberger and his wife and smiled coldly.

"I just wish I knew why you two are so afraid."

He wheeled his pony and set it to a lope. He was anxious to reach Milt Gulick's place by mid-afternoon at the latest.

Gulick was waiting for Slocum. The owner of The Bench was sitting astride a big chestnut on a hill overlooking his ranch, with four or five mean-looking riders at his back. He was a bulky, powerful bear of a man with a head that seemed to have been screwed into his burly shoulders. As Slocum approached, Gulick put his horse down the slope to intercept him, his riders trailing along behind him.

Noting the belligerent scowl on each man's face, Slocum rode to meet them.

As Gulick pulled up alongside Slocum, Gulick's riders kept a respectful distance back. It was Gulick who spoke first. "Who're you, mister? You're on Bench land."

"John Slocum," he replied. "And I suppose you'd be Milt Gulick."

"That's right. And I suppose you'd be from the Lazy C."

"Yes. I thought maybe we could talk about an alliance," Slocum said, aware even as he spoke that more than likely he was about to engage in another fruitless conversation.

"Alliance? Against who?"

"Slade Banner."

Gulick grinned suddenly, revealing a fine, brilliant smile. "Maria's had a falling-out with her ramrod, eh? Two pirates at swords' point over a division of the spoils." He chuckled. "I like that."

Slocum said, "It is not like that at all. Maria never knew until a few days ago what her ramrod was up to."

"And you believe that, do you?" Gulick snorted.

"I do."

Gulick looked at Slocum for a long moment, his eyes almost twinkling as he considered his response. "I reckon that young beauty has had her way with you, young man," he commented wryly. "And I guess I should envy you, but I don't. Not when I see how easily her undeniable charms have turned your brain to oatmeal."

Slocum should have been angry at that remark, but there seemed to be absolutely no malice in the man's words.

"How did you know that Slade and Maria are at odds?" Slocum asked suddenly.

Only then did Gulick become evasive. He shrugged his massive shoulders and said, "A little bird told me."

Slocum frowned. Why, he wondered, did Gulick hedge now? What made him want to hide from Slocum how he had learned of Maria's trouble with Slade? A sudden, prickling wariness fell over Slocum. He realized that there must be more to Neuberger and Gulick's refusal to throw in with Maria than simple animosity based on past experience.

Remembering the momentary fear he had seen in Neuberger's eyes and witnessing now the obvious reluctance on Gulick's part to admit what he knew, it occurred to Slocum that both ranchers were in some kind of a bind—a vise, perhaps.

If so, it was a vise being tightened by one Slade Banner.

"Slade Banner got to you first," Slocum said calmly, "didn't he, Gulick? What has he threatened to do if you back Maria and the Lazy C?"

But the man had his composure back by this time. "Forget it, Slocum," he said easily. "Ride on back into the arms of Maria. Then, if you're smart, you'll take her and that Mex out of this unpleasantness.

Her days here in this valley are over. She's a cattle queen no longer."

There was a hint of pain in Gulick's voice, the sad feel of something lost. It was Maria, Slocum realized in surprise. Gulick must be in love with her.

"Don't be too sure Maria's beat, Gulick," Slocum told him as he turned his horse back onto the trail. "I'll be back. That's a promise."

With a wave, he moved on past Gulick and his men and lifted his pony to an easy lope. He was not all that anxious to reach his next stop, the hill ranch belonging to Slim Hennessey, but he was determined to do what he could to get help for Maria's forces. He glanced at the sky as he rode. He would not reach the Bar O before sundown.

Slim Hennessey's Bar O was set against the face of a bald foothill ridge. A hidden spring fed a stand of cottonwoods at its base. Among these cottonwoods lay the careless scatter of the Bar O's buildings: a single-story log house, a low-roofed bunkhouse, pole sheds, and a corral.

In the gathering twilight, a hapless air of neglect hung over the place. The porch in front of the main house sagged dangerously, and in the front yard sprawled an overturned buggy with three of its wheels missing. A grindstone lay on its side, its shaft rusting. The place spoke of poverty, shiftlessness, and indifference.

Slocum had almost reached the log house when Slim Hennessey stepped through the open door, a rifle cradled in his arm. He was a tall, unshaven man in his mid-thirties with a tangle of dark, uncombed hair above his sun-darkened face. He had the slack, meager look of a man who drinks most of his meals.

"Now who the hell might you be?" he asked.

Slocum pulled up. "You mean you don't know?"

The man smiled, revealing yellow, broken teeth. "No, I don't, but if you don tell me soon, I'm liable to blow your damn fool head off, ridin' in here like that without a by-your-leave. This is Bar O land, and I'm the one who owns it."

"I'm John Slocum."

"That don't mean nothin' to me." He spat and shifted the rifle in his arm. As he looked at Slocum, his eyes narrowed dangerously, his face turning almost reptilian. "I think maybe you better just ride on out of here, mister."

"I'm from the Lazy C," Slocum said wearily.

"That so?" Hennessey spat again.

"Maria Coleman thinks it would be a good idea for you and the other ranchers in the valley to join her," Slocum went on.

"Join her? For what? And since when does she figure we're good enough for her?" Slim sent another dagger of tobacco juice at the ground. "And how come she didn't send Slade?"

"Slade Banner has broken with Maria and taken most of the Lazy C riders with him."

The man smiled. "And now Miss High and Mighty wants help from Slim Hennessey! Well, if that don't beat all!"

"She is serious. Slade has threatened to burn her out. If he does, and if he succeeds in driving Maria from the valley, you'll all have to deal with him on your own terms. That may not be so easy."

Slim grew cautious. "You asked the other ranchers yet?"

"Yes. I have just come from The Bench and the Bar N."

"What'd Neuberger and Gulick say? They throwin' in with the Lazy C?"

"They're thinking about it," Slocum lied.

Slim straightened and appeared to relax some. He let the stock of the rifle rest on the floor of the porch. "Light and set a spell. We got some talking to do, I'm thinking."

Wearily, Slocum dismounted and dropped his reins over the rickety hitch rail in front of the house, then followed Slim into his place. He almost wished he hadn't. The interior was smoky and close, the fetid air tainted with the smell of unwashed clothing and the dizzying stench that emanated only from the body of an unclean human.

The stove was thundering with a fresh load of kindling, a battered coffeepot on it spouting steam. The sink was piled high with dishes. Potatoes were spilling out of a corner. Beside them a sack of flour leaned against the wall, and white footprints radiated out from it into the kitchen and the sitting room beyond. Everywhere Slocum looked he saw litter.

Slocum had the sickening illusion that he had stumbled into the lair of some wild animal. Then he corrected himself. No wild animal would soil its own nest. It took a human being to live in this kind of filth.

Ignoring the steaming coffeepot, Slim lifted an earthen brown jug up onto the table, placed two tin cups down before them, and filled both. The moonshine blasted down Slocum's gullet like kerosene to which someone had just touched a match.

"Drink up!" Slim cried, holding the jug out to fill his cup again.

Through watery eyes, his brain already on fire, Slocum downed the moonshine and held his cup out for more. He cleared his throat and looked at Slim.

"You willin' to join us in stopping Slade Banner?" he asked.

"If you think you can stop that son of a bitch. He owns the law in this valley, you know. And he owns Coleman Flats, too. He's a very big man in these parts, Slocum. You go against him and you got trouble. How many riders at your back, not counting the Bar N and The Bench?"

Slocum shrugged. "Ten, maybe."

"And how many you think the Bar N and The Bench will bring with them?"

"I don't know."

"Well, I can tell you. Not all that many, and that's a fact."

"How many men do you have?"

"Two, besides myself."

Slocum nodded. He hadn't seen any sign of Slim's ranch hands when he rode up, and the place certainly gave the appearance of not having much help about. The Bar O would not be much of an addition to Maria's small force, but it might be just enough to convince the other ranchers to go along.

"Will you join us, then?" Slocum asked.

"Let me drink on it," Slim said, filling his cup.

It was remarkable, but the moonshine appeared to have no effect at all on Slim Hennessey, except to make him more alert, perhaps. Slocum got somewhat shakily to his feet. He had ridden through the entire day without once stopping to eat.

"I guess I'll be riding back," he said.

"What's the hurry, Slocum? Don't you want to know my decision?"

"Send one of your riders to the Lazy C when you make up your mind," Slocum told him.

He turned and started blindly for the door. It had suddenly become absolutely imperative that he flee the cabin's gut-wrenching stench. He was almost to the doorway when he found it blocked by Will Bright. There was a big, happy smile on Will's face. At the same time, what must have been Slim's rifle barrel came down on Slocum's head.

Slocum felt himself crashing through the floor into oblivion.

10

Slocum woke up with his head pounding. He didn't know if it was from the blow on the head or the moonshine. Both had been equally devastating in their effect. He sat up and rubbed his head. The smell of hay and horse manure was all around him, but wherever he had been flung, there was no light at all. He might as well have been dropped into a mine shaft.

Then it came again—the faint scratching sound that had awakened him. He reached out. His hand hit a sack of something and grain spilled out of the top and down his arm. He was in one of the barn's grain rooms. Standing up, he groped toward the sound and felt a rough board, then what appeared to be a door.

The scratching came again. At first Slocum had thought it might be a rat. But this time he heard his name called faintly. No rats he knew were able to do that.

"Who's there?" he called softly.

"Mr. Slocum!" a girl cried. "It's me, Mandy!"

"Mandy! What in blazes are you doing out here?" he asked.

"Will you help me?" she pleaded.

"First things first. Get me out of this room."

"It's locked from this side with a padlock," Mandy told him.

"All right. Go find a crowbar or something else you can use to pry off the latch."

He heard her scurry off and waited with his body leaning against the door. He was still shaky, and his head was pounding like someone was using it for an anvil, but he did his best to ignore that. After what seemed like a generation, Mandy returned.

"Mr. Slocum?"

"Did you get a crowbar?"

"Yes. But . . . I can hardly lift it."

"See if you can push it under the door."

She tried at three or four places, then succeeded finally in pushing its snout under the door and into the room. Groping blindly in the dark, Slocum caught hold of it and began to tug at it from his side. But he could get nowhere with it. Angry, he stood up and stomped with all his might on the floorboard under it. The rotten board gave way instantly and Slocum was able to pull the crowbar into the room.

"Stand back," he told Mandy.

After waiting a moment for her to get out of the way, Slocum began to pry apart the door. On his third heave, the nails holding the latch to the door frame squealed as they were pulled from the timber.

The lock and hasp thumped to the floor and the door sagged open.

Slocum stood silently in the doorway for a moment or two to see if the noise had aroused Will Bright or Slim. But all he heard coming from the house was drunken laughter, followed by the sound of something breaking, then more laughter.

Mandy hurried to his side. "They'll be coming for me again," she said miserably. "Please! You must get me away from here, Mr. Slocum."

He tried to calm her down. "Don't worry. I'll get you out of this. But what in tarnation are you doing here, Mandy?"

"I'm here because of you," she said miserably. "Will Bright was going to use me as a hostage to get you to come here. Only you just walked right in without him even having to contact you."

"You want to repeat that?"

Mandy told him the whole story. Will Bright had taken her from her apartment and forced her to ride all the way out here to Slim Hennessey's ranch. The two men used her all that afternoon. Shuddering miserably, she recounted their behavior. She felt soiled, ruined utterly. If she could, she would tear out both their hearts.

Slocum shook his head. "And the reason Will took you out here was because he thought you and I were lovers, which meant I'd be sure to come out here and rescue you. Then he would kill me."

"Yes," she said. "That's what he wants—to kill you for what you did to his brother."

Slocum nodded. In a way, he could not entirely blame the man.

Mandy looked at Slocum suddenly and frowned. "Would you have come for me, John?"

He put his arms around her, drew her close to him, and held her for a few minutes. Her trembling ceased and she relaxed against him. Smoothing her long blonde hair, he said softly, "You're damn right I would have." Then he kissed her tenderly on the lips.

She sighed. He could tell his words made her feel much better. It didn't matter if what he said was true or not, just so it was said. It was what she needed to hear. But in this case Slocum was not just telling the girl what he wanted to hear. He meant every word.

"Go on," he said gently. "Tell me the rest of it."

"When you rode in, you took Will and Slim completely by surprise. Will was in the barn keeping me quiet while you rode up. The same thing happened when Tim rode up earlier."

"Tim?"

"The hostler who works in the livery in town."

"He runs errands for Jenny, doesn't he? What in blazes was he doing all the way out here?"

"He had a message from Slade."

"Do you have any idea what it was?"

She nodded. "They made no effort to keep what the note said from me. Slade is offering to give Slim some of the Lazy C's cattle so long as he backs him and does not throw in with Neuberger and Gulick. And there was something else—something Slade's already threatened to do if Neuberger and Gulick back the Lazy C."

"What was that, Mandy?"

"I'm not sure, John. I just heard the two of them laugh and say what a real son of a bitch Slade Banner was if he was crossed. I think it had to do with some debts those ranchers owe to the feed store and the general store. Something about not letting them get any more credit and having to stay out of Coleman Flats. I guess Slade owns just about everybody and everything in town, at that."

"And you think Tim delivered this message to those other two ranchers before he reached here?"

She nodded. "Tim claimed Mrs. Neuberger would not even let him drink from her outside pump after she read the note he handed her husband. She just about ran him off with a shotgun," he said."

"Mandy, why have they left you out here like this? And why didn't Will kill me when he had the chance?"

"I have a place in the loft," she told him bitterly. "They stuffed a dish cloth in my mouth and tied me to a beam, but I got loose. They don't want to kill you until tomorrow. They are going to tie one of your feet to your pony's stirrup, then whip the horse so he'll drag you all the way back to the Lazy C."

Slocum shuddered in spite of himself. There would not be much left of him after such a ride, and it would look like an accident.

"Where's my pony?" Slocum asked her.

She indicated a stall in the back. He hurried to it and found the pony, still saddled. It looked very weary. The animal had obviously not been taken care of by anyone. Slocum found a bucket and sneaked out to the pump. The laughter from the house sounded vicious. The moonshine had turned the two men ugly and they were arguing bitterly about something. Hurrying back to the barn, he watered the pony, then grained it.

"Sorry I can't take off that saddle and rub you down, boy," he told the animal softly as he checked the cinch, led the pony out of the barn, and tied it up behind the house.

Beside him, Mandy said, "I can't ride a horse, John."

"Then you'll just have to ride up behind me and hang on," he told her.

"If I go back to Coleman Flats, Will won't let me rest. He'll always be after me."

"I'm taking you to the Lazy C, Mandy. You'll be safe from Will there."

She breathed a sigh of relief.

A harsh bark of laughter filled the night. It sounded much louder than before—as if the two men were standing in the house's open doorway. It would not be long, Slocum surmised, before the men would tire of the house and decide to visit the barn to torment their captives.

"Stay here," he told Mandy.

Slipping back into the barn, he searched for and found a kerosene lantern. Lighting it, he hurled it high into the loft. It took only seconds for the hay to catch. With a low *whump* of appreciation, like a genie freed from a bottle, the flames swept through the loft.

As the fire flared above him, Slocum ducked back out of the barn and around behind the house. A shout came from the house almost immediately. As the two men rushed across the compound toward the barn, Slocum remembered something and asked Mandy where the two hired hands were.

"They quit weeks ago," Mandy told him.

"Hell! The odds are better than I thought, then. Keep low, Mandy. I'll be right back."

While the two men plunged into the barn in a frantic effort to save their horses, Slocum ducked into the house and found his .44 and the Winchester he had brought with him. His bag was lying on the floor in a corner. He looked swiftly through it and found most of his possibles intact. Slinging the bag over his shoulder, he flung the nearest lantern against a wall, then picked up another lantern and let that fly as well. At once the walls became alive with climbing sheets of flame.

Not even the fires of hell could burn away that awful stench, Slocum thought as he climbed through a rear window and dropped beside Mandy and his pony.

"Up you go," he told her, grabbing her by the waist.

But he never finished. Someone's head slammed into his back, throwing him forward. He managed to twist himself around a moment before he went down and saw his attacker was Slim. As Slim aimed a kick at Slocum's head, Slocum reached out and grabbed his ankle, then twisted. Slim went down heavily on his back.

But he was up again instantly, head down, charging Slocum once again, aiming for his gut. Slocum stepped to one side and brought a knee up into Slim's face. Slim grunted and slammed back against the house. Flaming cinders from a window beside them sprayed down over Slocum as Slim braced himself against the side of the house, then launched himself at Slocum. Slocum drove a boot into Slim's shin. Slim staggered and started to go down. Slocum brought his knee up into the man's face again, with all his weight behind it.

Slim landed flat on his back, hard. This time he didn't even try to get up. Straightening, Slocum heard Mandy scream. He turned and saw Will just as Mandy flung herself at him. Will fired. The bullet meant for Slocum caught Mandy in the back. She cried out and slumped against Slocum.

Slocum caught her with one hand and drew his .44 with the other. He fired at Will, but the shot went wild. Will turned and ran off toward the blazing barn. A second later, he galloped out of the firelit compound. But Slocum paid no attention. He would see to Will later.

In the dancing flames that were now poking through the roof of the house, Slocum saw the extent of Mandy's wound. The round had entered her back under her right shoulder blade, ranged through her lung, and emerged just under her left breast in as jagged and ugly an exit wound as he had ever seen. If Mandy were lucky, she would die quickly.

Slim began to groan. Slocum put Mandy down carefully, went over to Slim, and kicked him hard.

Slim's eyes flickered open painfully.

Slocum bent over the man. "Now listen to me, Slim. I want you to clear out of this valley. For your own good. If I ever see you again after tonight, I will probably kill you."

Slim nodded hastily, then glanced past Slocum at Mandy. "Will do that?" he rasped painfully.

"Yes."

"I'll go," he said. "Soon's I get my possibles."

"Do it now," Slocum said brutally.

Grimacing painfully, Slim got to his feet. His face was ruined, his nose broken, one eye closed. Blood was already caking on his unshaven chin. He staggered off into the cottonwoods where he and Will had taken the horses they had rescued from the barn. By this time the fire had just about finished the barn, while from the house great whipping tongues of flame lapped at the sky.

Slocum went back to Mandy and carried her away from the searing heat, placing her down gently on the cool night grass. As Slim galloped off, she opened her eyes and looked up at him.

"Kiss me," she said softly, "the way you did in the barn. It was so gentle, so sweet."

He bent over her and kissed her again. Before he was done, she was dead.

11

It was late the next morning when Slocum found the spot he had been looking for on a knoll overlooking the broadest reaches of the valley. Above the valley, a smoky purple in the distance, hung the snow-tipped peaks that flanked it. The scent of sage and wild peppers hung in the air. A moment before, Slocum had seen a doe step cautiously from a patch of timber just below. The song of a hermit thrush echoed.

With a shovel he had rescued from Hennessey's ruined barn, he dug a grave and lowered Mandy's body into it. He had wrapped her in his slicker. To prevent wolves or coyotes from digging her body up, he piled stones upon the grave, constructing in the process a cairn all who passed by would recognize as such.

Then he doffed his cap and said a silent prayer for the girl who had saved his life.

• • •

Coleman Flats' single main street was quiet and watchful when Slocum rode in close to sundown. The hitch rack on one side of the street was empty, except for one hip-shot pony tied there. To the hitch rack on the other side of the street were tied maybe a dozen or so horses. Clots of men on both sides watched Slocum as he rode past. Many of them were Lazy C riders, Slocum had little doubt. The men watched him as he rode past, and Slocum returned their stare as he swung his pony toward the hitch rail in front of the Horse Head.

Before he reached the rail, Will Bright, flanked by Slade Banner and the sheriff, stepped out of the saloon and came to a stop on the low porch. Will's iron was low on his hip, his right hand hovering above it like a nervous bird.

Slocum pulled up. "Howdy, Will," Slocum said.

The fellow did not answer. He just let his hand drop a shade closer to the butt of his six-gun.

"You killed her, Will," Slocum told him. "Mandy O'Brien is dead. That bullet you meant for me found her. I buried her this morning."

Will shifted unhappily. Clearing his throat, he rasped, "That's your fault. If you hadn't rode in here like you did, none of this would've happened."

"I see. That's how you look at it, is it?"

"Ride out, Slocum," said Slade, speaking up suddenly. "We'll let you do that. Just ride on out of this valley and leave this business with the Lazy C to us. This is our valley. We've lived here for many years. We don't need outsiders like you to come in here and butt in."

"You say you'll let me ride out?"

"You heard me."

"That's real decent of you. But then maybe you know how difficult it would be for you to do anything else."

"Maybe."

Slocum appeared to relax as he considered the option Slade was offering him. Then he said, "What about Will here? You think he will let me go? Besides, maybe I should stay on. It looks like this might be a chance for me. Like it was for you, Slade."

Slade's eyes narrowed. "What do you mean by that, Slocum?"

"I mean you must have ridden in just like I did." Slocum glanced around at the town. "From what I hear, you've managed to turn quite a tidy profit since."

"And maybe you'd like some of that?" Slade asked carefully, sensing a deal. He appeared to have relaxed some.

"I been riding a long ways myself. Maybe it's time I settled down."

"And you think this valley can hold both of us, do you?"

Slocum shrugged. Then he looked at Will. "Not while Will Bright draws a breath in it. I want him to go—boots up or ass high. It don't matter much how he goes, just so he goes."

"You can't tell me what to do!" Will cried.

Slocum looked at him patiently. "If you don't go, I will kill you, Will. I don't want to have to do that.

I figure one brother is enough. I understand how you feel about the death of Jimmy, so I'm willing to let you go for the killing of Mandy O'Brien."

"Take his advice, Will," said Slade, pulling away from him. The sheriff pulled back also. "Slade's giving you a chance to save that fool ass of yours. Take it."

"You must be crazy!" Will cried. "We can gun down this son of a bitch right now! We got all this firepower and he's just one man!"

Slocum nodded amiably. "That's right enough, Will," he said, his voice deceptively soft. "I guess I might have some trouble killing you, but I'll get it done. Course, with all that firing, a few shots might go wild and hit Slade or the sheriff. And, sure, I'll take a few slugs myself, but you can bet your narrow ass that before I go down I'll have you dead."

"He means it," said the sheriff nervously, edging away from Will.

"Get on your horse, Will," said Slade, his voice cold. "Move out! Now!"

"Holy Jesus, Slade!" Will cried. "We got guns all around this bastard!" The man was beside himself with frustration at this sudden, inexplicable turn of events. "You can't do this, Slade!"

"I'm doing it!" Slade told him.

Will spun to face Slocum, clawing for his iron. But he never got his six-gun clear of leather. Slade and the sheriff swiftly pinned his arms to his sides. Slade lifted Will's weapon from its holster and handed it to the sheriff. Then he shoved Will from him with such force that Will almost fell to the ground.

"Get on your horse, Will!" Slade told him. "I ain't gonna tell you again!"

As he spoke, he rested his right hand on the butt of his own six-gun. Face beet-red, trembling with rage, Will Bright pulled himself together, flung one last, murderous glance at Slocum, then limped across the street toward the livery.

Slade glanced back to Slocum. "Light, Slocum, and come inside. Maybe you and me can deal."

Slocum nodded and dismounted. Dropping his reins over the hitch rail, he followed Slade and the sheriff into the Horse Head. Behind him the Lazy C riders still loyal to Slade streamed in. Watchfully, silently, they found places at the bar and at tables. Slocum could feel their eyes on him, like a ring of wolves on a winter's night.

As the sheriff found a table nearby, Jenny Warren set whiskey down before Slocum and Slade, then joined them, smiling across the table at Slocum. "Nice to see you again, Mr. Slocum," she said. What she meant was, 'You're lucky to be alive, Mr. Slocum.'

"Sounds like you want to deal," Slade said to Slocum. "That right, Slocum?"

"Depends on the deal."

"I'll make it as sweet as I can. You keep out of the way while I make my move against the Lazy C and I'll let you stay in this valley. Hell, I'll even give you Slim Hennessey's spread."

"That's hardscrabble country up there. Short grass and little water." Slocum grinned thinly. "And someone burnt the place down—the house and the barn."

Slade leaned back in his chair and regarded Slocum narrowly. He knew now that Slocum was willing to deal. The question was, what would it take to satisfy him?

"Hell," he drawled, "I would think a man like you would be able to pull that place together. I could let you have a couple of hundred head of Lazy C cattle, to give you a start. And that's good horse country, too."

"I'd prefer the Bar N. Good grass and plenty of water."

"You got a point there. Thing is, Neuberger'd likely want to hold on to his place."

Slocum smiled.

Slade looked quickly at Jenny. Her nod was so slight as to be barely visible. With a shrug, Slade nodded to Slocum. "Guess maybe that could be arranged, at that. Neuberger and that wife of his never would stand for me running cattle on land next to theirs. Gulick would be a problem, too."

"All right," said Slocum. "It's a deal."

Slade leaned forward then, his eyes narrowing. "There's just one thing bothers me. How come you ain't so hot to save Maria from me and my men? She give you trouble, did she?"

"I saved her bacon. You know how. But when I wanted a nice thank you, she pulled rank on me. It didn't sit well."

Slade accepted that. "She's an uppity gal, and so is that Mex. But, according to Will, you was still trying to get help for her when you showed up at Slim's place."

Slocum shrugged. "A man drops his line in where he thinks he might get lucky. Until he finds a better spot, that is."

Slade nodded, satisfied.

"How do you plan to finish off Maria and that Mex?" Slocum asked. "It shouldn't be too messy. The news might get beyond the valley."

Slade smiled. "Simple. We'll just starve them out. Drive off their herds and the rest of their livestock, raid their stores, then pull out. Keep them on that ranch until they run out of food and patience. No need for any bloodshed."

Slocum nodded.

Jenny spoke up then. "Besides keeping out of Slade's way, mister, what else are you going to give Slade for all this landscape?"

"And for me letting you live," Slade added with a smile.

"Help," said Slocum.

"I'm listening," Slade said.

"That Carvalho is no fool. He wasn't hurt too bad, and he's probably up and about already. He's got his men looking sharp, I'll say that for him. You won't find it so easy to ride in there and ruin their stores or run off their livestock. What I can do is make it a hell of a lot easier for you."

Slade's eyes lit appreciatively. "Go on."

"I'll create a diversion. A fire. One of their barns, maybe, or their storehouse. The Lazy C hands will be so busy with that, they won't have any time to stop you or put up any resistance. I'll see to that."

Slade's eyes met Jenny's. Slocum saw agreement between them.

Slade glanced back at Slocum. "It's a deal."

"There's just one thing," Slocum said.

"What's that?"

"I want this in writing. The entire deal. Including your promise about Neuberger's place. Let's call it a contract."

Slade leaned back in his chair. "You mean my word is not good enough for you?"

Slocum smiled sadly and shook his head. "I'm afraid not, Slade."

Jenny spoke up then, quickly, so as to keep things amiable. "I can write it out," she said to Slade. "There's no trick to that. Let's go into the office."

With a shrug, Slade got to his feet and followed Jenny as she led the way to her office. Slocum followed them in. As Slade closed the door behind them, Jenny went around behind her desk, sat down, and pulled some foolscap from a drawer. She reached for a pen and a bottle of ink and began to write.

Slade watched her uneasily, glancing occasionally at Slocum. Slocum could tell he didn't like this development, and was going along with it only because Jenny seemed to think it was all right.

Finished, Jenny glanced up, blotted the paper, then handed it to Slade. He glanced at it, made a pretence of reading it, then handed it quickly over to Slocum. In that instant, Slocum realized that Slade could not read—or, if he could read, it was only at a most rudimentary level. This made it clear to Slocum why Jenny had such a hold over him and why she had joined them at the table.

Slocum looked down at the document and read it quickly. The language was most impressive. For services rendered, Slocum was to be given the ranch now occupied by Sam Neuberger, the Bar N, as soon as Slade Banner regained the Lazy C, and the Bar N became available, at which time Slade promised to present to Slocum five hundred head of Lazy C cattle in addition to whatever stock came with the Neuberger holdings. The contract was binding on both parties for the next six months. A place for Slade's signature, Slocum's, and for the witness was at the bottom of the contract. The witness, obviously, would be Jenny Warren.

Slocum glanced at Jenny. "I see there's no mention here of how we plan to restore Slade's control over the Lazy C and to get the Bar N."

Jenny smiled. "I thought we would leave that to the imagination."

"Good idea." Slocum reached for her pen, dipped it into the inkwell on her desk, and signed. Then he handed the pen and the contract to Slade. He scrawled his name carelessly above Slocum's. Then Jenny took it from Slade and carefully signed her name as the witness.

Then she folded it and placed it in a bottom drawer she had to open with a key. When she closed the drawer on the contract, she locked the drawer and then dropped the key into the top drawer.

"When do we move?" Slocum asked Slade.

"How soon can you manage that diversion?"

"I should be back at the Lazy C some time tomorrow. How about the day after, at night? Say, close to midnight. There'll be a full moon that night—give you all the light you need."

Slade grinned. "Don't forget the light you are going to provide. We'll use it as a beacon. We won't move until we see it."

"Close to midnight, then. Don't panic if I'm not on time. It'll take some doing to get loose to set the fire. And I want to be sure I can ride clear after I set it."

"Like I said, we won't move until we get your signal. And we'll give you at least until one or two o'clock. But I would prefer it sooner."

"Around midnight. Count on it."

Slade stuck out his hand. Slocum could avoid it no longer. He took Slade's hand and shook it heartily. This seemed to relieve the man considerably. He grinned at Jenny. "Looks like we can move soon."

"Fine," Jenny replied. "This town is overrun with Lazy C hands. They're wearing out my girls and drinking all my whiskey. Coleman Flats needs a rest."

"We'll put them to work soon enough," Slade promised, escorting Slocum to the office door and pulling it open for him.

Slocum touched the brim of his hat to Jenny, said goodbye to Slade Banner, and left the saloon. The Lazy C ranch hands followed him out and watched him mount up. Not a word was spoken. As Slocum pulled his pony around and lifted it to a quick lope, their eyes watching him felt heavy on his back.

A moment later, as the town vanished behind him, he shuddered. He felt as if he had just climbed out of a nest of vipers.

12

Later that night back in Colman Flats, Slocum heard a sound behind him and whirled. A shadowy figure loomed out of the alley's darkness. Slocum could not tell if the man had drawn his weapon. Ducking behind the outhouse, he flattened himself against its side.

"Hey! That you, Pete?" the fellow called softly, pulling up. "Where the hell you been?"

The outhouse door swung open and a man stumbled out, buttoning his fly as he came. "For Christ's sake, Andy, what's the hurry?"

Andy lurched across the alley toward his companion. He stumbled once in the darkness before reaching him.

"Hey, wait a minute," said Andy. "Who was that just ducked behind the glory hole? Wasn't that you, Pete?"

"You're seeing things!"

"No, I wasn't."

"Come on! Them two floozies still waiting on us?"

Andy muttered something. Pete laughed and dug his partner in the ribs. Sniggering merrily, the two men turned about and stumbled off.

Slocum waited until they had both disappeared into the night before he stepped out from the behind the outhouse and continued on down the back alley. It was well past midnight, but some cowboys, evidently, never knew when to quit.

The Horse Head Saloon was dark. Slocum found the window leading into Jenny's office. It was not locked. He lifted the sash and eased himself over the window sill, then crouched down beside the window to listen. There might be someone still in the saloon. Jenny and Slade, maybe, drinking to their new partnership with John Slocum.

Hearing nothing, Slocum moved on cat feet across the room to the door. He had removed his spurs before starting down the alley. Pressing his ear against the door, he listened for a while longer. The only sound came from the street out front as a horse and rider galloped past.

Slocum's eyes had adjusted to the room's darkness by now. He moved across to the desk and felt in the top drawer for the key to the bottom drawer. It was not there. He swore and took a match out of the waterproof tin he carried. Striking it, he held the tiny flaring torch over the desk.

The key was right in front of him, gleaming in the match's light. Slocum shook out the match and snatched up the key. In a moment he had the bottom drawer open. Reaching in, he found the contract. The heavy paper on which it had been written was still impressively stiff and new. Holding it up to the dim light filtering in the window, he was just able to make out his signature and those of Slade and Jenny.

Refolding the contract, he placed it in the breast pocket of his jacket, then closed the drawer, locked it, and placed the key back where it had been, on top of the desk. Returning to the window, he dropped to the alley floor, pushed down the window sash, and moved swiftly back up the alley. His pony was tethered at the far end of it behind the feed mill. Slipping on his spurs, he mounted up and rode unchallenged out of town, heading north toward the Bar N.

His hope now was that neither Jenny nor Slade would feel the need to take out the contract and inspect it before Slade made his move on the Lazy C.

Still cradling his shotgun, Neuberger stood with his wife on the porch as Slocum rode in. The Bar N ranch hands were also in sight, peering at him from various vantage points about the compound. This time all of them were armed.

Pulling to a halt in front of them, Slocum smiled and touched his hat brim to Samantha Neuberger. "Howdy, ma'am," he said to her. "You still got any of that coffee left?"

"I have a fresh pot on the stove," she snapped at him. "Always do. But you're not welcome to any of it."

"What are you doing back here, Slocum?" Neuberger asked. "You got your answer already. We are not throwing in with the Lazy C."

"I got something to show you," Slocum replied.

"And what might that be?" the rancher asked.

"A contract."

"What?"

Slocum dismounted, dropped his pony's reins over the hitch rail, and mounted the porch steps. As he did so, he reached into his inside pocket and drew forth the contract.

"Here it is," he said, handing it to Neuberger. "Read it for yourself. You too, Mrs. Neuberger."

It took only a second or two for Neuberger to read it. Astonished, he handed it to his wife.

"I'd like an explanation, Slocum," Neuberger said.

"It has been a long ride. Through the night, in fact. That fresh coffee would go good about now. Then I would be glad to explain."

Samantha thrust the contract angrily at Slocum. "Come inside," she snapped. "You are a strange man, Mr. Slocum, to come here so brazenly with such a document in hand."

"Yes, ma'am," he said, following the woman into her immaculate house.

Once the coffee was poured and the three of them were sitting at the deal table, Slocum commenced his explanation.

"I obtained that contract from Slade Banner by promising to help him subdue the Lazy C. He thinks I am now working for him, that I will do what it takes to enable him to take the Lazy C from Maria Coleman. He has promised—as this contract makes clear—to give me the Bar N ranch in payment for my services."

"But that makes no sense!" Neuberger protested. "The Bar N is not his to give. Not to anyone!"

"Not now, it isn't."

"Then what . . ."

"Slade Banner is thinking about taking over this entire valley after he gains control of the Lazy C. He will own the town and the biggest spread in the valley. What little law there is up here is on his side, no matter what he does. It is clear that he intends to use that power to get what he wants. And if he wants to pay me off with your ranch, why, that is precisely what he will do."

"Why, Slocum? Why are you telling us this? Why did you come here with that contract?"

"Don't you see, Sam?" his wife asked. "It's Mr. Slocum's way of warning us about Slade Banner."

Slocum nodded grimly at Samantha Neuberger. "That's it, ma'am. I figured maybe it would help you to see things a bit clearer if you knew what Banner was up to. Maybe now you'll see the wisdom of throwing in with the Lazy C."

"But if we help you," Neuberger protested, "Slade will ruin us."

"He'll ruin you either way. Seems to me you have only one way out of this."

"To fight him," Samantha said.

"Yes. Join the Lazy C and fight him. And I have

a plan. With it, I think we have a good chance of stopping him."

The rancher looked at his wife. She took a deep breath and nodded.

Neuberger looked back at Slocum. "Tell us your plan."

"Later. Right now, I want you to ride over to The Bench and convince Milt Gulick to throw in with us. We'll need him and his men. If he argues, show him this contract, and explain it to him the way I did to you. Remember this; if Slade is planning to drive you off your land and give it to me, he'll be just as willing to deal away Gulick's spread when the time comes."

"Do it, Sam," said Neuberger's wife. "Milt will listen to you."

"As soon as you can, by tonight at the latest, bring Milt with you to the lazy C. I'll explain my plan then. To be on the safe side, before you leave your spreads, I suggest you drive into the hills whatever horseflesh and breeding stock you value, just so it's out of Slade's reach for the next couple of days."

Neuberger nodded grimly. "I'll see to it at once."

Slocum finished his coffee and got up. "Thanks for the coffee, Mrs. Neuberger."

She smiled, and in that instant her plain, careworn face looked surprisingly radiant. "Call me Samantha, John Slocum. I think we're going to be friends."

"Partners, at least," agreed Neuberger, getting to his feet and picking up the contract.

A nearly exhausted Slocum got into his saddle a

SLOCUM AND THE CATTLE QUEEN 147

moment later and turned his pony toward the Lazy C. Glancing back, he waved. Standing together on the veranda, Sam Neuberger and his wife waved back.

"What's that?" Slocum asked, sitting up suddenly.

"A bathtub, John," Maria told him. "The other ranchers will be here soon. You have slept through most of the afternoon. Don't you think it's about time for your bath?"

"Yes," he admitted, scratching his gritty scalp. "I guess I must be pretty rank by this time, at that."

Little Raven and Maria placed the tub down at the foot of his bed. It was some tub, not at all like the big corrugated steel tubs Slocum usually frequented in the back rooms of barbershops. This one had obviously been picked out by Maria for her own use. Its enameled surface was decorated with painted blossoms and roses, and it had a graceful, flaring backrest, from which hung a towel rack.

Little Raven hurried out.

"Hadn't you better get undressed?" Maria asked regarding him impishly.

With a sigh, Slocum stood up, unbuttoned his shirt, and took it off. Then he peeled off his britches and stepped out of his long johns.

"Oh my," Maria said softly, staring at his crotch. "All that was . . . inside me?"

"All of it."

Without once glancing at Slocum's naked body, Little Raven began lugging in steaming buckets of water and dumping them into the tub. When the tub was full, Slocum stepped into it carefully, relishing the feeling of the steaming hot water as he slowly sank down into it. Beads of perspiration popped out on his forehead. He could almost feel the encrusted dirt lifting off his skin.

"Close the door, Raven," Maria said. She knelt on a cushion beside him. She had a long-handled brush in one hand and a bar of yellow soap in the other.

"I can wash myself," Slocum told her, reaching for the soap.

"I know you can," Maria said. "But you did me a favor, so now I am going to do you one."

At once she began soaping his head. Stinging suds flowed down his forehead into the corners of his eyes. He blinked painfully, but kept his composure. Abruptly, Maria shoved his head forward, down into the hot, sudsy water. He pushed his head up, blowing like a whale. She laughed and pushed his head down again, keeping it there while she rinsed the soap from his hair.

He was gasping when she finally let him up. "You trying to drown me?" he asked, somewhat plaintively.

She just laughed. "You are like a little boy, I see. You don't like to have your hair washed."

"It's the drowning I don't like."

"Hush!" she said. "Close your eyes."

He shut them just in time as she picked up another bucket of steaming hot water and poured it over his head and shoulders. The shock caused Slocum momentarily to lose his breath. Gasping, he shook himself like a wet dog, and started to get out of the tub.

Laughing, she pushed him back down, reached into the steaming water for the brush and soap, and began scrubbing his back.

This was more like it. He sighed happily. He glanced at her and saw that she was making no effort to hide her pleasure in the contemplation of his broad shoulders or the ribbed muscles of his chest as she scrubbed up over his shoulders and down his front.

All the way down.

"Ah . . .!" she murmured. "It's so big!"

As she leaned forward, her strong fingers closing mischievously about his erection, her flushed face came close to Slocum's. Without conscious volition, he fastened his lips upon hers. She moaned and leaned into him, her hand working expertly now. He put his steaming arms about her and clung to her. The rapid movement of her hand caused the water to splash up over them both, but neither paid any attention. Then he gasped and cried out, still clinging to her. She laughed, delighted, and let him lean back against the tub's backrest. Drained, he regarded her through lidded eyes.

"Stand up," she told him softly.

He got to his feet obediently.

"It seems I have diminished you," she commented as she soaped his thighs, the backs of his legs, his ankles, and his feet. "What strange power is this we women possess over you big, strong men?"

As soon as she had finished pouring another bucket of steaming hot water over him, he reached out, took her in his arms, stepped out of the tub, and dropped her onto the bed. He was still soaking wet, but she did not protest as he swiftly unbuttoned her dress and helped her remove her corset and shift. In a moment she was naked under him.

And he was no longer diminished.

Her arms encircling his neck, she drew him down onto her. As he entered her, she gasped in pleasure. "Ah, my stallion!" she whispered in his ear. "It still hurts, but it does not matter. Such sweet pain!"

He lay upon her, smiling down while she moaned in pleasure. He felt himself hard and sure inside her. He kept her impaled beneath him, intent on her face glowing up at him. She raised herself up to kiss him, softly and lingeringly.

"It's all in there," she whispered. "I can feel it!"

He ran his hand up her flank, then across the soft swell of her breasts. Under his palm her nipples came erect. Moaning softly, she let her head drop back and closed her eyes as she drank in the feel of what his hand was doing to her.

He began to thrust then, sure and steady, pausing slightly each time he struck bottom. She began to quiver in his arms, legs spread apart under him, breasts swelling against his chest, arms still clinging tightly around his neck, her eyes still closed. He allowed his pace to quicken. He heard her moan softly. The sound came from deep within her throat. Abruptly, without any hint from him, she lifted her legs and locked them around his waist as she began to arch up to meet each of his thrusts.

"Open your eyes and look at me," he told her.

Her eyes opened. Her gaze met his and held there, wide and dreaming, as he quickened the pace of his thrusting. She met each thrust now, her eyes still on his, her face taut with the intensity of her need. Faster and faster they rocked. They cleaved together now, one single pulsing entity, striving to reach higher and higher. . . .

Maria started to fling her head from side to side. Her fingers dug into his bare back. Then, uttering a long, arching cry, she climaxed. He groaned and wanted to cry out as well. The ache building within his groin reached a crescendo. He felt his seed tearing up through him as he drove on mindlessly, barely aware of her clinging to him, lost in his own sweet universe of pleasure.

He exploded, driving her down into the bed, holding his pulsing organ deep within her as he emptied himself in twitching, spasmodic pulses. The frenzy passed. A sweet calm came over him. He looked down at her then and smiled. She smiled back, wordlessly. Still inside her, still caught in the grip of her thighs, he dropped his face alongside hers on the pillow and drank in the intoxicating perfume of her hair, of her still pulsing flesh.

"Thanks for the bath," he muttered softly.

"Any time," she whispered, her teeth closing gently about his earlobe, her sweet breath warming his neck.

"You learn fast."

"You are an excellent teacher," she replied.

"You are an apt pupil."

"Tell me, is there more to learn about making love?"

"Yes, you lucky girl. You have just begun. There is a world of delights for you to explore. And you have a lifetime ahead of you to devote to this exploration."

"Mmm," she murmured, hugging him close. "How nice."

They were about to drift off when Little Raven knocked at the door. Maria sat up at once. "What is it?" she called.

"The people you wait for," Little Raven told her through the door. "They come now."

"Have you let them in?"

"They just ride in."

"Tell Antonio. Have him greet them at the door, and tell them I will be down soon."

The sound of Little Raven's feet padding away from the door faded rapidly. Slocum sat up and rested his head against the pillows. Maria turned her head and smiled at him, then let her head rest back against his chest. Slocum closed his hands gently over her breasts.

"I'll need some time to get dressed," he told her.

"And you should shave as well. I will make excuses for you and send Raven up with some fresh clothes. My father was about your height and build, though he did not have your shoulder breadth."

Dressing swiftly, she kissed him lightly on the lips, then slipped through the door. A moment later,

Slocum heard the sound of masculine voices raised in greeting as Maria descended the stairs. Slocum lay back on the bed, stark naked, crossed his arms behind his head, and waited for Little Raven to bring him fresh clothes.

He had not slept more than a few hours before Maria had awakened him. Before that he had ridden through the previous night, and indeed, all told, he had spent better than twenty hours in the saddle. After all that, he had been called upon to do even more riding.

Yet he felt fine.

The door opened and the impassive Indian entered, her arms piled high with clean long johns, pants, and shirt. Without a glance at him, she placed them down on the bed beside Slocum and left.

Slocum watched her leave, then began dressing with a shrug. Hell, what did he expect? He couldn't charm every woman he met.

13

Slocum used the large dining-room table to illustrate his plan. As he placed everyone about the table, he found himself recalling his days in the Confederate Army. He hoped that singular and bloody experience would serve him well now.

Ben and Neuberger stood at his side, Gulick, Carvalho, and Maria across the table from him. Using salt shakers, cups and saucers, the sugar bowl, and the cream pitcher, he swiftly and deftly created a miniature landscape. Knives and forks helped for boundaries. Imagination did the rest.

"Let's say this is Coleman Flats," Slocum said, indicating the sugar bowl and the cream pitcher. "And here we are, across the valley." A cup sitting facedown served to represent the Lazy C. "These salt and pepper shakers are the hills above the town where Slade has left the rustled cattle."

Slocum glanced at Ben. Ben cleared his throat and looked around at the others. "I just got back. The cattle are still there, with only a couple of Slade's men herding them."

Slocum looked back at the others. "That means we can use them."

"How?" Milt Gulick wanted to know.

"I'll get to that later. Now, let's start at the beginning. As I have already told you, Slade is making his move tonight. Some time around midnight he expects me to set one of Lazy C's outbuildings on fire. This was my suggestion. I convinced him that everyone would be so busy trying to put out the fire that the ranch would be left wide open for Slade's attack."

Neuberger spoke up then. "Then that burning building will be his signal to attack?"

"Yes."

"You mean you are going to set fire to one of our buildings?" Carvalho demanded.

He was standing beside Maria, pale but erect. Despite his weakened condition and Maria's pleas, he had insisted on joining this night's battle.

"No, Señor Carvalho," said Slocum. "I have already had the men pile up some old lumber and fence posts behind the barn, along with anything else that will burn. Gulick and his men will douse the pile with kerosene and set it afire a little after midnight. From a distance it will look as if the barn itself is on fire, and will draw Slade and his men into your trap."

"You won't be here?" Maria asked.

"Neuberger, Ben, and I will be in the hills north of Coleman Flats."

"Maybe you better explain that," said Neuberger.

"Let's deal with Slade's attack on the Lazy C first. His intent is to destroy the storeroom and run off all the livestock and horses. After that, he plans to pull back and wait. He feels starving out Maria, Señor Carvalho, and the rest of the Lazy C riders will be less bloody than storming in and cutting them down—and a whole hell of a lot safer."

"That son of a bitch," Gulick said softly.

"But you and your men will be waiting for Slade, Milt," Slocum told Gulick. "You can pick him and his men off as they ride in." Slocum placed some silverware down in a parallel formation on the tablecloth at what represented a few miles' distance from the ranch. "They'll ride up through this draw, most likely. It's the most direct route, and will put them in the middle of that pasture where Slade expects to find your breeding stock and the rest of Lazy C's livestock, including the horses. If you place your men so they are flanking his route to the storehouse, Slade and his men should get it both coming and going."

Gulick smiled. "We'll let them ride through the draw before springing the trap," he said, nodding happily. "Then we'll tear them apart when they flee back the way they came."

"Good," said Slocum. "Señor Carvalho, I suggest, would make a fine second in command."

Gulick looked at Carvalho. "You will be in charge of protecting the barn and the storehouse, in case any of Slade's men should get through," he told him. "And you will see to the lighting of the signal fire."

Carvalho nodded.

Slocum looked across at Carvalho. "Just don't let your men open up before Slade has swallowed the bait."

"You do not have to remind me of that, Señor Slocum."

"What about me?" Maria asked.

"Just stay out of danger," Gulick said, speaking for Slocum.

"I could light the fire," she said.

Gulick smiled at her. "Yes," he said, "you could do that. You could set the bait before them."

Pleased, Maria looked back at Slocum. "Will that be all right, John?"

"Yes. But, like Milt just said, stay out of danger."

"Of course."

Neuberger cleared his throat impatiently. "I still don't understand our role in all this, Slocum," he said. "Why are we going into the hills north of Coleman Flats if all the action is going to be back here at the Lazy C?"

"Because all the action is *not* going to be back here. After he is driven back from the Lazy C, Slade and the majority of his men will make a run for the town. After all, his force should outnumber ours considerably. From my observation, most of the men hanging around the town are outlaws of one stripe or another—gunslicks on the run. I have no doubt Slade will enlist their services as well. Besides that, he owns most of the town." Slocum glanced at Gulick. "Even the Horse Head Saloon. Isn't that right, Milt?"

"It's a fact," Gulick said bluntly. "Jenny Warren's just fronting for him, same as Potter and Phillips."

"So if we cannot match him man for man, we can at least cut him off from his base, destroy his nest entirely. Give him no place from which to mount another attack on the Lazy C or any other ranch in this valley. Wipe him out completely. The mill, the general store—everything."

"And are we going to do that?" Neuberger asked.

"That is my plan. We're going to gather up that cattle he has left north of town and stampede them through the town. During the confusion, we will then fire the place, raze it completely. We will then turn about and meet Slade's forces as they stream back to Coleman Flats."

"A pincers," commented Gulick approvingly. "With us snapping at their rear and you at their front."

"Exactly. And when his forces scatter, there will no place for Slade to run."

"If all goes according to plan," Carvalho said softly.

"Yes," Slocum agreed, glancing across the table at the Mexican. "If all goes according to plan." He straightened then and looked about him. "We haven't much time. Now let's attend to the details."

Soberly, gesturing occasionally toward the miniature world he had created on the tablecloth, Slocum began to go over, in much greater detail, the battle plan for stopping Slade Banner.

• • •

A little before midnight, Ben came alert, then stood up in his stirrups. Pointing suddenly, he said to Slocum, "Over there!"

Slocum looked where Ben indicated and saw Slade and his men emerging from a patch of timber. In the bright wash of the full moon, he could almost count each rider as they streaked across the valley floor on a beeline for the Lazy C. His guess had been a good one. Slade's force numbered at least eighteen riders, considerably more than if he had limited himself only to those Lazy C riders who had remained with him.

For a moment Slocum suffered misgivings. Slade's considerable numbers were riding against a force that contained only eight men, including one weak though very brave old Mexican. The only thing that consoled Slocum was the knowledge that, in battle, surprise was worth a great deal.

And there sure as hell was a surprise in store for Slade Banner.

Slade and his men disappeared. Slocum turned to Ben and nodded. The two riders put their horses off the ridge and a moment later pulled to halt on a small, moonlit benchland, where Neuberger and three of his riders were waiting. Below them in a narrow moonlit swale were the stolen cattle the loyal Lazy C riders had just finished rounding up. Slocum could see the Lazy C cowboys still riding slowly around the herd, doing their best to settle the cattle down.

"Any trouble?" Slocum asked Sam Neuberger.

"One of Slade's men pulled his iron, but he decided not to fire it when he saw how many riders there were surrounding him. The other drover offered no resistance at all. He was just pleased to keep his scalp."

"Where are they now?"

"Hog-tied over there," Sam said, pointing to a small stand of timber on the other side of the swale. "In among those trees. They should be able to wiggle loose some time tomorrow, we figure."

"Good enough." Slocum took a deep breath. "Well, let's go, then."

With Slocum in the lead, the six men angled down the slope into the swale and pulled up around the Lazy C cowboy Slocum had put in charge of this midnight roundup.

"Spread your men out," Slocum told him. "We're moving out now. Remember, we don't want a stampede until we get to the outskirts of town—and I want these cattle to go right down the main street, then back again if need be."

The rider nodded, pulled his mount around, and galloped alongside the herd to one of his outriders. A moment later, a chorus of ragged whistles filled the night, a few unhappy cattle began to low, and then the heaving backs started moving in a dark, massive wedge toward the meadowland below.

Jenny Warren swore softly. Then she straightened up and swore again, this time louder. The drawer was empty. The damned contract was gone.

Swiftly, she looked about the office, as if in doing so

she might be able to find some trace of Slocum still hovering in the shadows. She went to the window. It was shut, but not tightly, the sash not quite snug against the sill. He had gotten in this way, then. She wondered how long ago, then realized it did not matter.

Before Slade rode out that night, he had suggested that it might be a smart move for Jenny to tear up the contract before she went to bed. When this was all over, if Slade had anything to say about it, it would be a cold day in hell before he let Slocum take over a ranch in the valley. Jenny shook her head. Slade had been right on target. The trouble was that it looked uncomfortably like John Slocum was at least one step ahead of them. She shivered slightly. Her fortunes were tied to those of Slade Banner, and she now had a disturbing premonition that Slade might be riding into a far more treacherous battle this night than either of them had realized.

She bent and closed the drawer, then locked it needlessly. She was about to drop the key onto the desk when she heard the first faint rumbling beneath her feet. She reached out and took hold of the desk. To her surprise, it was trembling slightly. A picture on the wall by the door shifted slightly, and the rumbling sound, like that of an approaching train, grew even louder.

Could it be an earthquake? She was frightened. She had never been in an earthquake and had heard terrifying stories about them. The rumbling reached a crescendo. Abruptly, above the thundering, heart-constricting rumble, came the bawling of bleating cattle.

She ran from the office and out through the saloon. As she passed the bar, whiskey bottles began toppling off their shelves and crashing to the catwalk behind the bar. She paid no attention as she flung herself out through the batwings.

What she saw astounded and terrified her. The street was filled with a bellowing tide of maddened cattle. Even as she took this in, one wild-eyed steer, swept along by the bawling, stampeding brutes at its back, climbed up onto the Horse Head porch and charged blindly at Jenny. She ducked swiftly back into the saloon and took refuge behind the bar as the steer lowered its head and charged through the batwings after her, taking a sizable portion of the doorjamb with it.

Other steers followed the lead of this first one and began pouring through an ever-widening hole in the side of the saloon. Once inside, the frantic brutes began milling wildly, reducing chairs and tables to splinters. The stream of crazed steers soon became a torrent. The entire wall facing the street buckled, the windowpanes shattering, sending tiny shards of glass over the floor. Some of the pieces stuck to the sweating backs of the cattle as they continued to mill about in the cramped saloon. By this time not a single bottle remained on the shelves, and as the steers continued to butt insanely at the bar, Jenny felt it begin to shift dangerously.

Ned Riley and Chips—the first her bartender, the other the house gambler—were halfway down the stairs. Both men were still in the act of dressing. One was slipping into his pants, the other pulling on his boots. Behind them, peering fearfully around the balustrade, were two of Jenny's girls.

"What's going on?" Riley called down to Jenny.

"A stampede! Can't you see that?"

"But where in hell did these cattle come from?" Chips demanded.

For a moment Jenny was as baffled as they were— until she thought of Slocum.

"John Slocum!" she cried angrily. "Get your weapons and round up as many men as you can. That son of a bitch Slocum is using these cattle to take this town!"

At that moment Jenny saw that one of the steers had found its way to the rear and was in the act of crashing through to the alley beyond. She reached down under the bar for the shotgun and a handful of cartridges. Levering swiftly, she began firing over the heads of the cattle. Frantic, eyes starting out of their heads in panic, they started climbing each other in a desperate effort to escape. Jenny fired again, moving out from behind the bar this time.

The cattle plunged away from her, saw the opening at the rear of the saloon, and charged for it. Before long, the cattle were running in a steady, bawling stream through the saloon and out into the alley beyond. Dropping two more cartridges into the shotgun, Jenny waited for a break in the stream, then darted out onto what was left of the saloon porch and fired point-blank at the first steer headed her way.

It veered away, plunging and leaping over the

backs of those nearest it. Another steer being swept toward the porch needed convincing also, and Jenny fired. The animal swung away, taking the rest of the maddened throng with it. Reloading swiftly, Jenny stood her ground, occasionally sending a shot at the stampeding cattle to keep them going past the saloon.

Ned Riley and Chips pulled up behind her on the porch. She glanced back at them. Both men were strapping six-guns to their waists.

"Tell the girls to stay put," Jenny told them. "Then go find Potter and the sheriff. Get all the men you can. We've got to be ready when Slocum shows."

They nodded and vanished back into the saloon.

Jenny turned back to the stampeding cattle. As she did, her heart skipped a beat. Farther down the street, the general store was ablaze, the garish flames leaping from its windows adding to this insane night still one more dimension of terror. The flames drove the animals to a further frenzy. Wide-eyed, heads lifted as they bawled in terror, they swept on past the blazing building, some so anxious they were attempting to climb over the backs of the slower brutes in front of them.

The porch Jenny was standing on shifted, then crumbled as the heavy bodies sweeping past finally wore away its last support. Jenny was frightened now as the brawling, plunging torrent veered closer to her. She fired twice over their heads, but it helped only a little. She dug into her dress pocket for shells and found that she had no more. With a tiny cry, she flung the shotgun aside and ducked back into her ruined saloon.

166   JAKE LOGAN

* * *

"There goes the barn!" Slade cried to Mel Floren. "Slocum's keeping up his end! Let's go!"

Turning in his saddle, he waved to his men, then turned back around and clapped spurs to his mount, leading them off the ridge toward the draw that would put them in the middle of the Lazy C's back pasture.

As he dipped below the benchland ahead of him, he kept his eye on the glowing sky and chuckled. The layout of the Lazy C's ranch was as familiar to him as the palm of his hand. He knew where every outbuilding was, including the storehouse and those chicken coops in back. Hell, they might as well take care of the coops while they were at it—torch them, too. And the blacksmith shop. Maria Coleman would be a sad but wiser woman when this night was over.

And she would be eager for a deal.

Slade, still out in front of his men, Mel Floren just barely keeping up with him, was through the draw first. As he broke into the meadow below the main barns, he did not see what he had expected. There were no horses or colts, none of the breeding stock he would have expected, no cattle either. The fields gleamed in the bright moonlight, but they were unnaturally empty. He strained his eyes to see if any stock had gathered under the few clumps of cottonwood which dotted the undulant grassland.

But he saw nothing, and for the first time felt slightly uneasy.

Ahead of him, the flames from the burning barn were leaping high into the night sky. The barn itself stood out clearly against the flames, remarkably solid despite the raging inferno that was now sending a shower of flaming embers high over the Lazy C compound.

Damn it, the barn was not on fire!

Beside him, Mel cried, "I don't like this, Slade! That fire don't look right!"

Slade agreed with him. Something was wrong. Then he realized what it was, and swore. Slocum had double-crossed him. The barn was not on fire. The flames were coming from behind the barn.

"Pull up!" Slade cried, as he reined in his mount. "Pull up! It's a trap!"

At once, rifle fire broke out on all sides. Slade felt a slug whisper past his cheek and saw Mel pitch forward over the neck of his horse. Dismounting swiftly, his six-gun drawn, he knelt by Mel's side and saw the man gasping for breath, a thin trickle of blood streaming from the corner of his mouth. There was a jagged hole in his chest.

Beside Slade, his horse whinnied pitiably and collapsed as a bullet caught it in the chest. Ducking to one side, Slade fired at a muzzle flash in the deep grass, then swung into Mel's saddle and pulled his horse around.

His men had pulled up, demoralized by the unexpected fire. He galloped back to them and rallied them, pleading with some, shaming others, urging them to follow him toward the Lazy C compound. "We aren't finished yet!" he insisted. Then, wheeling his horse back around, he led his men back toward the ranch, the storm of riders on his heels trampling the dying Mel Floren into the bloody ground as they swept past.

"There they are!" cried Maria to Antonio. "Over there! Behind the barn!"

Crouching down behind the corral gate, she watched as Slade Banner led his riders past the bonfire she had lit and on toward the Lazy C compound. Milt Gulick's men opened fire from the barn and the storehouse behind Maria, but Slade's men kept coming, spraying lead at the muzzle flashes as they rode.

By this time the gunfire was a constant rattle as the defenders poured a steady fusillade at the onrushing riders from every corner of the compound. The problem was that there were two riders for every defender, and, as Slade's men poured into the compound, they seemed invulnerable to the defenders' fire.

Maria could hold herself back no longer. Standing up, she aimed her Winchester at one of the lead riders. Tracking him carefully, she fired. The man peeled backward off his horse. Stifling a triumphant cry, she levered a fresh round into the firing chamber, picked out another rider, and squeezed the trigger. This shot missed, however, and the rider, his six-gun blazing, swung his mount in her direction.

"Get down!" Antonio cried.

He stood up and pushed her roughly down behind the corral. Startled by his roughness, Maria looked up angrily at Antonio and was just in time to see the old man stagger. It appeared to Maria as if someone had just slapped him a little too heartily on the back. Antonio sagged to the ground.

With a cry, Maria dropped her rifle and knelt beside him. Antonio coughed painfully and reached up to grab Maria's arm. "You see! You must keep down, Maria!"

"Oh, Antonio!" she cried. "I am so sorry! Are you hurt bad?"

He smiled up at her. "It is all right, my child. My time has come."

"No, Antonio! No!"

The sound of approaching hooves filled the night. Maria glanced up to see Milt Gulick beside her, his six-gun out. Aiming swiftly, Gulick fired at the oncoming rider. The rider slumped sideways off his horse. The sound of his heavy body striking the corral fence was sickening. His riderless horse veered sharply away from the corral and galloped after the rest of Slade's men.

Milt Gulick knelt beside Maria and Antonio. "How is he?"

"Antonio has been hurt bad. The bullet struck him in the back."

Gulick bent close, placing his ear next to Antonio's mouth. Then he rolled the man over and quickly examined the wound. He looked up at the stricken Maria. "He is dead, Maria."

Sobbing, Maria buried her head in Milt's chest. He held her close and did his best to comfort her as Slade and his riders cut raggedly toward the compound gate, leaving at least four dead or wounded men in their wake.

Watching him go, Gulick felt a mean satisfaction. Slade did not know it, but he had still another gauntlet to run—the draw. Gulick had left his men to see to the battle here at the compound, and he was glad, at least for Maria's sake, that he had. But the bulk of his men were waiting now to pick off still more of Slade's bunch as they fled back through the draw to Coleman Flats.

In a moment he would gather up the defenders and pursue Slade until he met Slocum's force coming from the town. But that would have to wait for a few seconds longer, he realized as he comforted the heartbroken girl who still clung to him.

As the last of the stampeding herd swept through the town, Slocum stepped into what was left of the Horse Head Saloon. He was just in time to see a distraught Jenny Warren disappear into her office. Drawing his six-gun, Slocum followed her.

She spun about at the sound of his entrance. "You!" she cried.

"It's me, all right."

"You double-crossed us!"

Slocum smiled. "Before you could double-cross me."

"You won't get away with this. Slade won't let you," she sputtered.

"That has yet to be settled, Jenny."

"Damn you to hell, anyway! Let me out of here!"

As she started to leave the room, Slocum blocked

the doorway. "There's just one thing I'd like to know, Jenny. How did Slade know when those trail herds from Oregon were due—and how did he know which routes would be taken?"

"You think I'd tell you?"

With a reluctant shrug, Slocum fired at the kerosene lantern on Jenny's desk. The bowl shattered, sending kerosene over the desk and the wall beside it. The flaming wick, fluttering like a moth, struck the wall. Instantly, a sheet of flame swept up it as far as the ceiling.

Shielding her face from the ferocious heat, Jenny looked with terror at Slocum.

He smiled. "Yes, Jenny. I think you'll tell me."

"All I know is there's someone who tips Slade off. After each trail herd is . . . diverted, Slade has to set some money aside to pay him."

"His name?"

"I don't know it!"

Slocum crossed his arms and leaned back against the door. Acrid clouds of black smoke were hanging just below the ceiling now, and most of the wall and a good portion of the ceiling were on fire. Slocum could hear the cries of the girls on the second floor.

"I want his name," Slocum repeated.

"I don't know it, I told you. Please! You must let me out of here! I can hear the girls!"

"Let me refresh your memory. Could his name be Chino Smith—a small, ratty-looking fellow with mean eyes?"

He had taken her by surprise. Eyes wide, she exclaimed, "Yes, that could be him! Once I heard

Slade call him Chino. I'm sure of it. And he always showed up not long after Slade got another herd."

Satisfied, Slocum uncrossed his arms and stepped aside. Jenny darted past him from the room. He followed out after her and stood close by the ruined front wall as Jenny herded her girls down the stairs and out through the smoke-filled saloon.

As they hurried across the street, Slocum followed them and saw Sam Neuberger emerging from the restaurant. Flames were leaping in the window behind him and smoke was pouring from the alley. Slocum and his men had not waited to follow in behind the cattle, but had infiltrated the town from both sides even as the herd was stampeding through it. Now, up and down the street, several buildings were on fire. Already the mill and the general store were nearly gutted.

From down the street a shot rang out and a round ricocheted off the porch post beside Slocum. Neuberger darted into an alley, and Slocum did likewise. The sheriff and three other men emerged from a smoking building farther down the street, firing as they came.

Crouched beside the remains of a crushed water barrel, Slocum began returning the fire as other townsmen emerged from the flaming ruins, guns out and firing. Neuberger returned fire from the alley as the rest of Slocum's force, having waited patiently for this moment, began firing from various vantage points up and down the street.

The battle was joined.

A moment later, Slocum saw the sheriff go down,

then found his own spot getting a bit too hot and ducked back deeper into the alley. His intention was to get around behind a couple of men firing at Neuberger from a storefront a few blocks down the street. He was in a hurry to bring this fighting to a decisive finish. Before long, he and his men were due to close the other jaw of that pincer on Slade's fleeing forces.

As Slocum reached the back alley and started to run along it, he heard a thunder of hooves growing behind him. Startled, he looked back and saw a cloud of horsemen galloping toward him through the smoke. He was about to duck into a doorway when he recognized the lead horseman. It was Harry Johnson, the drover he had escaped from the other side of this valley. Beside Harry rode his ferret-faced partner, Chino Smith. And just behind him, a wide grin on his face, was Will Bright.

As the horsemen crowded about him, Slocum saw that Harry and Chino had him covered. Cocking his revolver, Harry Johnson grinned down at Slocum. He looked immensely pleased with himself.

"Once I found your trail on that ridge," he told Slocum, "I had no trouble following it to this valley. I knew I'd find you again, Slocum! This time you won't get away!"

"Raise your hands!" ordered Chino Smith. "And don't make no sudden moves!"

Slocum was about to tell Harry once again that he was mistaken. But he had been through all that before. For a second or two he didn't know whether to laugh or to cry.

Then he shrugged wearily and held up both hands.

14

"I told you he was here!" cried Will Bright. "Let me finish him for you. He killed my brother."

"Hold it," said Harry, turning on Will. "Just hold your hosses, mister. I want to know what's going on around here. How come this town is in flames? Whose cattle was that stampedin' through the place?"

"That was your cattle, Harry," said Slocum. "What was left of them, that is. Slade Banner sold the culls to a buyer this past week."

Harry frowned back down at Slocum, almost as if he were disappointed in him. "Then you admit it was you and this Slade feller who rustled that herd?"

"Why not, Harry? You got your mind set on blaming me," Slocum said. He slowly lowered his hands and smiled up at Chino Smith. "Okay, Chino, take his gun. Slade'll be here before long with your cut."

Chino did not know what to say or do. He looked

swiftly at Harry, then back at Slocum, in an agony of indecision. It was evidently occurring to him for the first time that maybe he had misjudged Slocum, that, despite what Will must have told him, Slocum *had* been working for Slade all this time.

"Hurry up, Chino!" snapped Slocum. "Take Harry's gun!"

Perspiration popped out on Chino's forehead. It could have been the heat of the burning buildings on all sides of them or his own terrible uncertainty. But Slocum's command tipped the balance against Harry.

Cocking his six-gun, Chino said, "Sorry, Harry. Give me your gun. You heard Slocum. I would've had to do this sooner or later. I warned you. I tried to keep you out of this valley. But you just wouldn't listen."

Furious, realizing for the first time the treachery of his sidekick, Harry handed Chino his weapon. There was a murmur from the riders encircling them, but as he took Harry's gun and stuck it into his belt, Chino glanced around.

"Stay back," he told the riders. "Every damn one of you—or I'll kill Harry!"

The drovers stirred unhappily in their saddles, then, muttering, moved their horses back cautiously.

Overhead, the night sky was alive with flaring cinders, while the air in the alley was growing denser by the minute as black coils of smoke drifted lower and lower. Slocum's eyes were beginning to burn painfully. When he saw Chino reach up suddenly to wipe at his own eyes, he leaped forward, slapped

Chino's gun to one side, then dragged the man from the horse.

Chino clung to his gun, however, and swung it up like a club, catching Slocum in the gut. Slocum doubled over, gagging. Another blow on the back of his head sent Slocum down onto one knee. Reaching up, he tried to wrestle the gun from Chino's grasp, but Chino just ducked back, grinning.

"Hold it right there!" screamed Will.

Groggily, Slocum looked up and saw Will's six-gun trained on him. Chino, fully recovered now, was once again holding his weapon on Harry Johnson. There was a hint of madness in Will Bright's face as he looked down his barrel at Slocum.

Harry Johnson's men were confused. They had seen Slocum's attempt to get at Chino and its failure. Though some of the riders muttered angrily and one or two hurled a curse at Chino, they were obviously afraid to do anything that might endanger Harry.

Harry glanced down at Slocum. "Thanks, anyway, Slocum. I guess I had you all wrong from the beginning."

"You did. The man you wanted was Chino. He was the one tipping off Slade Banner whenever a herd was on its way."

"This man, Slade Banner—you say he's the one behind all this cattle rustling?"

"He was the foreman of a ranch in this valley, the Lazy C."

"But why?"

"It was his way of stocking the ranch."

"Shut up, you two," said Chino nervously. He

turned to Will. "Okay, Will. Take care of your friend here. Shoot the son of a bitch. We can't stay in this damn burning town any longer. My eyes are about to pop out of my head."

Will aimed carefully down at Slocum.

But the shot, when it came, issued from the shell of a blackened building further down the alley. Will crumpled forward over his saddle horn. In his death agony, his twitching muscles caused him to squeeze off a shot. The round crashed into the ground at his horse's feet. The animal reared, throwing Will clear, and in the confusion Slocum hurled himself once again upon Chino.

Bearing the smaller man down under him, Slocum cuffed the man's weapon from his hand, straddled him, and began hammering at his face with both fists, each sledging blow causing Chino's head to snap around. After about the fifth such blow, Slocum felt Chino's jaw give way. Uttering a strangled cry of pain, Chino tried to crawl out from under Slocum. Slocum got to his feet, dragged Chino upright, then threw him at the feet of Harry Johnson's horse.

"There's your double-crosser!" he said. "Strap him to a horse!"

At once some riders jumped down from their horses and dragged the whimpering Chino away. Turning then, Slocum saw Ben walking up the alley toward him, a pleased grin on his perspiring face. At once Slocum knew it was he who had shot Will Bright. Behind Ben streamed Neuberger and the rest of his men.

Coming to a halt before Slocum, a weary, smoke-blackened Neuberger said, "The sheriff's dead, Phillips and Potter are wounded. The rest of the men rode out."

"What about Jenny Warren?"

"She's safe with her girls on the other side of town. The Chinaman who used to work in the restaurant is with them."

Harry dismounted and walked over to them. "Maybe you'd better tell me what's going on around here, Slocum."

Swiftly, Slocum explained to Harry Johnson why he and the others had turned Coleman Flats into an inferno and what still lay ahead of them this night.

When he had finished, Harry smiled. "You think maybe you could use some more men?"

Slocum looked up at Harry Johnson's riders. A few of them, those who had been so anxious to hang him a little more than a week ago, did not want to meet his frank, appraising gaze. The others grinned down at him.

Slocum glanced back at Harry. "Why not?" he said. "You fellers got a score to settle, just like us. Let's go!"

His riders strung out behind him, the Lazy C pursuers keeping close on their trail, Slade rode like a man possessed. It was riding back through that draw that had almost done him in. From all sides the fire had come, peeling at least three of his men off their horses. One bullet had ricocheted off his saddle horn. The sound of it was like the whisper of the devil as he cleared his throat before saying, 'Welcome, friend. It's about time.'

Well, as sure as bears shit in the woods, Slade was going to return to the Lazy C. Once he reached the safety of town, he would lick his wounds for maybe a week and let Jenny pamper him some. Then he would come down on the Lazy C with all he had. He would stomp them all! Torch their buildings, scatter their livestock!

But first things first. Right now, he had to shake free of his pursuers, after which he would tend to that bastard Slocum. Oh, how he ached to send a load of buckshot into that big man. And he would! He would see to that. He would scour the valley for him!

It was close to dawn, but as Slade rode he became confused. The light in the sky was coming from the wrong direction. Since when did the sun rise in the north? Then, looking closer, he saw how the light varied, becoming brighter one moment, then growing less intense the next.

Hell, that was no sunrise. That was a fire—a big one!

With a groan, Slade realized what he was seeing. Coleman Flats was on fire! That son of a bitch Slocum had fired his town! While Slade was at the Lazy C, Slocum had taken riders to Coleman Flats. But how could he have managed it? He didn't have that many men, and Slade had left the sheriff and at least ten good men behind.

Still riding hard, he saw with each passing second how widespread the glow was, and how complete the devastation must be. Holy Christ! He had no place to go!

The thought almost paralyzed him. For a moment he considered pulling up to get his bearings. Then he remembered that pack of Lazy C riders still on his tail.

"Slade! Look!" one of his riders cried.

Slade glanced back. One of his men was pointing off to the right. Looking in that direction, Slade saw a clot of riders top a ridge, then head for Slade and his men, fanning out as they came.

He was trapped. There were riders at his back, and what looked like at least ten or more coming at him head-on.

"Keep going!" Slade called to his men. "Blast your way through them!"

"Like hell!" a rider called. "I'm giving up!"

"Me, too," said another. "I've had enough!"

Slade spun about in his saddle and saw his men sawing back on their reins. Many of the horses were rearing up, their forelegs pawing at the air, so abruptly were his men coming to a halt. Slade turned his mount and cut to the left, heading for the mountains.

He rode hard and well, and once he had slipped through the mouth of the pincers, he let his horse out and was soon climbing into the foothills.

Only one rider was on his tail. And Slade Banner knew damn well who that was.

Slocum came to a sluggish creek and forded it easily. Slade Banner's tracks were still deep in the soft sand beside the creek. A swarm of deerflies attacked

Slocum. He slapped furiously at them and continued into the foothills. Only when he had had traveled some distance from the creek was he free of the persistent little bastards.

He found himself in a rock patch of badlands, the grass scarce, the mountains sheer and tall, towering high above him. In places the striated walls blocked out the bright morning sky. Banner's tracks, however, remained clear, and Slocum was sure he was gaining on him.

By mid-morning he turned his pony into a dungeon-like defile that turned and twisted like a snake under overhanging and interlocking walls so high that Slocum could not see a speck of sky. The floor of the cleft was irregular, wet, sandy, and in places soupy. Banner's tracks were clear as newsprint.

At last the defile opened up and led out onto a wide, flat rock serving as the floor of a broad canyon. The stream that cut it was only a thin, sluggish trickle. And Slade Banner's tracks had vanished.

As Slocum quickly wheeled his pony and rode back toward the defile, a shot rang out from the canyon rim. The bullet ricocheted off a rock wall beside him. A moment later, Slocum reached the cover of the defile and dismounted. A quick, thorough search of the small interlocking canyon and deep cuts brought him at last to Banner's horse.

Banner was up there then—waiting.

Snaking his Winchester from its scabbard, Slocum levered a fresh cartridge into the firing chamber, then found a rough trail that appeared to lead up to the canyon rim. Clambering past the loose talus, he began to climb. It was close to noon when he reached the rimrock and started picking his way over the rocks and crevasses along the canyon's rim.

Slocum froze and flung himself down. He had caught the sudden gleam of sunlight on a rifle barrel in the rocks just ahead of him. Keeping as flat as he could, Slocum removed his spurs and pocketed them. Still keeping down, he snaked sideways along the ground so as to come at the rocks from another angle. He was almost to them when he heard the scrape of boots on stone as Banner moved about wearily. The sound came from just beyond a huge boulder. Smaller rocks flanked the boulder.

Getting to his feet, Slocum ran openly for the rocks. Banner heard him coming. Showing himself, he began levering his Winchester rapidly, sending a withering fire at Slocum. The air seemed alive with steel-jacketed hornets. Reaching the rocks, Slocum flung himself to the ground, digging his elbows and knees painfully into the rocky ground.

But he had made it. He had the protection of the rocks now. Banner fired a few more rounds, each one ricocheting harmlessly off, then went silent. Keeping low, Slocum inched upward among the rocks until he was above the boulder. He caught sight of Slade below him and fired. The round missed, but Banner spun about in panic, looking for a way out. What had been his citadel was now likely to become his gravestone.

Again Slocum poked around the boulder and fired. This time, Slade was waiting and loosed a steady fusillade from his Winchester, almost emptying the chamber. Slocum swore softly and ducked back as the bullets whined harmlessly off the rocks.

Banner ceased firing. Slocum took a deep breath, counted to ten,. and again flung himself up to fire. But Banner was no longer behind the boulder. Slocum darted from cover and clambered down the rocks to the boulder. He was just in time to see Banner slipping carefully down onto a narrow ledge below the canyon rim. When he glanced back and saw Slocum, Banner turned and jumped.

Slocum raced over and peered down at the ledge. Below it was flat rock that jutted out over the canyon floor. But in closer to the rock face Slocum caught sight of a trail leading back down the canyon. Slade Banner had leaped for the rock below the ledge. It was less than a ten-foot drop and should have given him no trouble. Unfortunately, he was still lying on the rock face, writhing painfully, his leg twisted crookedly under him. He had apparently broken it.

As Slocum peered down at him, Banner flung up his Winchester and fired. The round lifted Slocum's hat off his head. He ducked back, cursing his carelessness.

A sudden panting scream came from Banner.

Peering over, Slocum saw at once what had happened. In firing up at Slocum, Banner had flung himself backward. As a result, he was now continuing to slide backward over the rock's smooth, sloping rock face—as the gravel under his body carried him relentlessly closer to the edge.

"Help me!" Banner cried. "I'm going over! I can't stop!"

As he spoke, he flung his Winchester aside and started scrabbling frantically for something to grab hold of; but there was nothing. The rock was bare of all vegetation. As Slocum watched in grim fascination, Banner slipped closer and closer to the edge.

With a final, terrifying wail, Banner disappeared. His wail ended abruptly far below, its echo filling the canyon for a moment or two. Slocum glanced at the sky, searching its bright emptiness for the inevitable buzzards.

He saw only one. But that would be enough, he realized, as he turned and started back down to his pony.

Slocum smiled and mounted up. "Thanks, Maria," he said. "But no thanks. I've already spent more time than I should have in this valley. I'd like to keep moving on."

"That's what you've been saying for the past week, so I guess I have to believe you."

"You really don't have much choice," Slocum told her, still smiling.

It was a bright morning, and Slocum was ready to leave. The Lazy C was a more honest but far less prosperous spread than it had been when Slocum first came into the valley. Maria had given Harry Johnson back the herd Slade Banner had taken, and then some. It had been her way of evening the score.

Still, the Lazy C would be growing again soon. Slocum could see the way the wind was blowing. Milt Gulick's visits to the Lazy C had been for longer and longer periods, and now, whenever Slocum came upon Maria and Gulick discussing ranch business—or whatever it was they were discussing—Maria had a tendency to blush and Gulick to look uncomfortable.

Milt Gulick was standing beside Maria now, glowing. He was not at all unhappy to see Slocum go.

"Well, I guess this is goodbye, Slocum," he said. "The best of luck to you."

"Thank you, Milt."

Gulick reached up and shook Slocum's hand. The grip was firm and as strong as Gulick himself, his smile bright and filled with confidence. Yes, Slocum told himself, Maria Coleman could not do much better than this.

"Will you be staying over at Coleman Flats?" Maria asked.

"I wasn't thinking of it. The place is still pretty raw, I understand. I've decided to head south. I should get to that pass you showed me by nightfall."

"Oh, yes," Maria said. "I remember."

The memory of that pass warmed Slocum even as he spoke of it. The two of them had spent a wild night there during a picnic that had taken them all of three days to complete. That had been soon after the trouble with Slade was over, while Maria was still seeking Slocum out for the skills he taught so well.

"Kiss me goodbye, John," Maria said.

Slocum leaned down as Gulick, somewhat embarrassed, took a few steps back. Moving up onto her tiptoes, Maria kissed Slocum lightly on the cheek.

Then, laughing softly, she whispered, "I'll say goodbye properly at the pass tonight. You remember that big cottonwood?"

"I remember," he whispered back.

Her dark, almond-shaped eyes glowed. "I'll be there."

Slocum straightened up and touched his hat brim to Maria. He waved to Gulick and turned his pony about. Ben was standing in the doorway to the blacksmith shop. The two men waved to each other. The rest of the ranch hands just watched. John Slocum had cut quite a swath through their lives and the life of this ranch, and they did not quite know what to make of him.

A moment later, lifting his pony to a lope, Slocum headed south across the valley floor. He should have felt bad, he realized, leaving still another warm and cozy harbor, but the anticipation of that proper goodbye coming up at the pass this night would not let him be sad.

He almost felt like chuckling—and, eventually, he did.

JAKE LOGAN

___ 0-425-06338-0	SLOCUM AND THE CATTLE QUEEN #57	$2.25
___ 0-872-16880	SLOCUM'S BLOOD	$1.95
___ 0-872-16823	SLOCUM'S CODE	$1.95
___ 0-867-21071	SLOCUM'S DEBT	$1.95
___ 0-872-16867	SLOCUM'S FIRE	$1.95
___ 0-872-16856	SLOCUM'S FLAG	$1.95
___ 0-867-21015	SLOCUM'S GAMBLE	$1.95
___ 0-867-21090	SLOCUM'S GOLD	$1.95
___ 0-872-16841	SLOCUM'S GRAVE	$1.95
___ 0-867-21023	SLOCUM'S HELL	$1.95
___ 0-872-16764	SLOCUM'S RAGE	$1.95
___ 0-867-21087	SLOCUM'S REVENGE	$1.95
___ 0-872-16927	SLOCUM'S RUN	$1.95
___ 0-872-16936	SLOCUM'S SLAUGHTER	$1.95
___ 0-867-21163	SLOCUM'S WOMAN	$1.95
___ 0-872-16864	WHITE HELL	$1.95
___ 0-425-05998-7	SLOCUM'S DRIVE	$2.25
___ 0-425-06139-6	THE JACKSON HOLE TROUBLE	$2.25
___ 0-425-06330-5	NEBRASKA BURNOUT #56	$2.25

Available at your local bookstore or return this form to:

BERKLEY
Book Mailing Service
P.O. Box 690, Rockville Centre, NY 11571

Please send me the titles checked above. I enclose _____.
Include $1.00 for postage and handling if one book is ordered; 50¢ per book for two or more. California, Illinois, New York and Tennessee residents please add sales tax.

NAME _____

ADDRESS _____

CITY _____ STATE/ZIP _____

(allow six weeks for delivery)